"Tasma" (Jessie Cou........, ...gate, London in 1848. She migrated with her family to Tasmania in the early 1850s. In 1867 marriage to Charles Fraser took her to country Victoria, and the period up to her divorce in 1883 was marked by the launching of her career as a writer, and by two extended trips to Europe. In 1885 she married Auguste Couvreur, a prominent Belgian, and was subsequently based in Brussels. There she produced six novels, among them her immensely popular work, *Uncle Piper of Piper's Hill* (1889), and numerous articles and short stories, including *A Sydney Sovereign and Other Tales* (1890). She died in 1897.

Michael Ackland is a Senior Lecturer in English at Monash University. He has published widely on nineteenth-century Australian literature, as well as on American, English and Continental writing from the same period.

IMPR·INT
CLASSICS

A Sydney Sovereign

TASMA

Introduced & Edited
by Michael Ackland

Angus&Robertson
An imprint of HarperCollins*Publishers*

AN ANGUS & ROBERTSON BOOK
An imprint of HarperCollinsPublishers

First published in Australia in 1993 by
CollinsAngus&Robertson Publishers Pty Limited (ACN 009 913 517)
A division of HarperCollinsPublishers (Australia) Pty Limited
25-31 Ryde Road, Pymble NSW 2073, Australia

HarperCollinsPublishers (New Zealand) Limited
31 View Road, Glenfield, Auckland 10, New Zealand

HarperCollinsPublishers Limited
77-85 Fulham Palace Road, London W6 8JB, United Kingdom

National Library of Australia
Cataloguing-in-Publication data:

Tasma, 1848–1897
  A Sydney sovereign
  ISBN 0 207 18121 7
  I. Ackland, Michael, 1951– . II. Title.
A823.2

Typeset by Midland Typesetters, Maryborough, Victoria
Cover: John Longstaff 1862–1941 (Australian) Lady in Grey 1890
oil on canvas, 135 × 90 cm
Presented by H. Connell 1914
Courtesy of the National Gallery of Victoria
Printed in Australia by Griffin Paperbacks

CONTENTS

Introduction   vii
What an Artist Discovered in Tasmania   1
The Rubria Ghost   23
Robina's Awakening (from *A Sydney Sovereign*)   35
How a Claim was Nearly Jumped in Gum-tree Gully   41
Barren Love   59
A Philanthropist's Experiment   79
Monsieur Caloche   95
His Modern Godiva   117
An Old-time Episode in Tasmania   127
Notes   143

INTRODUCTION

1889 was a critical time in the life and literary career of Tasma. Both were poised on the threshold of momentous developments, following the great success achieved at the outset of the year by her first novel, *Uncle Piper of Piper's Hill*. Its well-drawn characters and the dramatic clash between Old and New World values won for her a transatlantic, in addition to an Australasian, readership. The bold steps she had taken over the past years to reshape her life were now bringing handsome dividends. In 1883 she had sought a divorce from her Australian husband, Charles Fraser, and in 1885 she had married the Belgian politician and eminent journalist Auguste Couvreur. Thereafter she settled down in Brussels to her most productive period of writing, that saw the composition of six novels as well as diverse essays and stories. This activity assured her of considerable, independent standing in her new milieu; however, fame also brought with it problems, as emerges from Tasma's diary entry from 11th January, 1889, which deals with a social gathering in the Belgian capital:

> *A lady (with a moustache next to me) hearing that somebody's books were being talked about, turned to me by way of being amiable, and said 'J'ai les femmes auteurs en horreur . . . Et vous madame?' I said 'Je le regrette Madame, parce que c'est justement de mon premier petit livre que Madame Berardi est en train de parler.' It would have made a famous thing one would rather have left unsaid, but it shows how backward the modern Bruxelloise must be. There is not an upcountry township in Australia where such a remark would be made.*

Although the exchange is amusing, it does underscore that with the appearance of *Uncle Piper* Tasma's battle to establish herself in the publishing world was by no means over. As the Belgian socialite's comment "I have a horror of women writers" indicated, there were still many who would need to be persuaded of her achievements. And Tasma knew it, despite the measured pride and irony which lend an unmistakable air of assurance to her rejoinder: "I'm sorry, Madame, but Madame Berardi is speaking actually about my own first, small book." In 1889 the pressing questions for her were what to turn to next to ensure her new-won standing, and how best to capitalise on what would prove to be the phenomenal popularity of her initial novel.

Tasma's response was to continue publishing, and to return to those themes and stories to which she owed her current standing. This selection spans much of her career. It reprints some of her earliest tales, all the pieces she chose to reissue immediately in the wake of *Uncle Piper*, and some of her new creations. Collectively, these works reveal the pre-occupations that shape her fiction, and carry the reader from the original, antipodean surrounds of the artist to the cosmopolitan environs in which she shone with such assurance in her later years.

Already the glittering salon of Madame Berardi, peopled with the social élite of Brussels, was a far remove from the writer's more modest origins. Born at Highgate, London, on 28th October 1848, Jessie Catherine Huybers had migrated to Hobart with her parents during the early years of the goldrushes. Here her father prospered for a time in business, while her mother Catherine, of Anglo-French descent, fostered a family interest in spoken French and in European culture. Jessie's serious writing career, however, dates from 1877, a decade after her first marriage. In that year various works such as "Malus Oculus," "Fable for a Rainy Day" and "Barren Love" appeared under the pen-name "Tasma". Other stories followed in steady succession, with the *Australasian* proving to be a ready outlet for manuscripts sent by this talented contributor, who lived south of Bendigo in the small township of Malmsbury. Experiencing the relative cultural isolation of the Victorian countryside, Jessie's thoughts would have been drawn irresistibly to what some of her later fictional characters refer to as the promised land of Europe. There were to be found the history, complex social fabric and intellectual monuments the fledgling colonies lacked, as well as the possibility of wider recognition. These motives, or similar ones, underlaid two major expeditions which she undertook to the Old World before her divorce: the first in 1873, the second in 1879. There she met in 1881 the man destined to be her second husband, and there during her second stay she was acclaimed as a public speaker and writer. Fame and perhaps fortune were now almost within her grasp—there could be no going back to the intellectual isolation and scorching summers of Malmsbury.

The years immediately preceding Jessie's second voyage to Europe saw the first printing of most of the tales which, a decade later, she would reissue hard upon the heels of her first novel in *A Sydney Sovereign and Other Tales*. This brought together "How a Claim was Nearly Jumped in Gumtree Gully," "A Philanthropist's Experiment" and "Monsieur Caloche," which had all appeared in the *Australasian* in 1878, and "Barren Love" from Garnet Walch's *"Hash": A Mixed Dish for Christmas* (1877). During this early period she had also contributed other short stories to the then-popular form of the colonial miscellany, including 'What an Artist discovered in Tasmania' to Walch's *Australasia: An Intercolonial Christmas Annual* (1878), and "The Rubria Ghost" to F. R. C. Hopkins' *The Australian Ladies Annual* (1878). With this considerable output, the aspiring author had provided proof of real talent and achieved local accreditation. She was ready to chance her hand in "fresh woods, and pastures new".

In setting her sights on a wider, overseas audience, Tasma was pursuing a familar path for Australian writers, and one on which she, as a woman, could justifiably hope for some measure of success. Writing on Anglo-Australian themes had long proved to be a viable undertaking, and earlier female authors, such as Mary Theresa Vidal, Ellen Clacy and Catherine Helen Spence, had found a receptive English market for accounts based on colonial life. More recently, another Victorian-based writer, Ada Cambridge, had begun to exploit Old World interest in colonial romances; and the waning decades of the nineteenth century would witness related works by writers such as Rosa Praed, Catherine Martin and Mary Gaunt. Thus, although there was undoubtedly an element of exaggeration in the private diary statement that 'there is not an upcountry township in Australia where such a [negative] remark would be made,' informing the entry is an awareness of the undeniable literary success attained there by "femmes auteurs". Society in Brussels, she seems to suggest, might pride itself on its inherited culture and *savoir-faire*. But this was not matched by a flexibility and openness to other and changing human needs, which were more readily accommodated in the less socially restricted theatre of the antipodes.

The reasons underlying Tasma's decision to publish a selection of her earlier writings in 1890 under the title *A Sydney Sovereign and Other Tales* were complex. Most obviously, she was hoping to profit from the appetite aroused for her distinctive style of fiction by the novel of the preceding year. Financial concerns also played a part, in spite of, or more accurately because of, the elevated social position she now enjoyed. As she confided to her diary at the outset of the 1890s, Auguste and she gave an impression of economic well-being that far outstripped their actual resources. Hers was, as she frequently noted, a Cinderella-like situation: "Book-making and carpet shaking with Rosalie in the morning and coming out in the evening in . . . unexpected splendour" (February, 1889). Furthermore, the financial return from *Uncle Piper of Piper's Hill* was meagre in comparison with its sales, and these combined factors made her anxious no doubt to issue a follow-up work as soon as possible. Finally, and most disquietingly, Tasma felt doubts about the continued sources of her inspiration. The proofs of *A Sydney Sovereign and Other Tales* were received in September 1889. Yet rather than exciting hopes, we find its imminent release generating unease and self-doubts on the last day of the departing year:

> *The new book*—A Sydney Sovereign—*with my early tales that Truebner has just brought out, is about to take its chance. May it be as successful as the first! I am the more anxious about these poor works of mine that I have a desperate misgiving as to the likelihood of producing any others. I am not sure that even the power remains.*

The ensuing years did little to dispel these misgivings. They were marked by rapid and voluminous composition, but never by a repeat of the success of her first novel. Moreover, the death of Auguste in April 1894, increased financial burdens, and constant worries related to her closely knit family all took their toll upon her, until her health gave way in 1897 at the age of forty-eight. She died after a slow, three-month decline from heart disease on 23rd October, and was cremated according to her wishes at Paris.

This modern selection offers significant insights into three distinctive phases of Tasma's career. The first is the critical period before her second voyage to Europe, which witnessed the initial flowering of her creative talent. This is represented by six short stories of late 1877–1878, in which Tasma honed her craft and found many of her abiding themes. She could then, with justice, present herself overseas as an Australian author of repute, and hope to build upon this promising career beginning. How justified or otherwise these hopes were may only now be assessed by a wider reading public, for this is the first time that these key works have been brought together. Furthermore, this is the first republication of the pieces which constituted *A Sydney Sovereign and Other Tales*. These are titles three to seven reprinted here, and appear in their original sequence. Only the first and title story "A Sydney Sovereign", which is a novella of 122 pages, is not reproduced in its entirety. Strictly speaking, it has no place in this current collection of short stories. It is represented, however, by a brief extract to give the reader some idea of the total form of the 1890 volume, and of the matter which immediately preceded the four reprinted tales from 1877–78. Finally, the selection closes with two works from her years in Brussels: a period of her shorter fiction writing which is largely unresearched. As "His Modern Godiva" from the *World* on 23rd July, 1890 and "An Old-Time Episode in Tasmania" from Harriet Patchett Martin's *Coo-ee: Tales of Australia by Australian Ladies* (1891) demonstrate, there was no observable weakening in Tasma's mastery of the short story genre. Whatever faults may have begun to beset her longer prose works at this time, her handling of the briefer form remained assured in its delineation of character, and in its development of a central problem.

Tasma's stories, despite their frequent local settings, are less concerned with the epic contest being played out between the colonists and the landscape of the New World, than with human interaction and motivation. Again and again her plots rely on extremes of character or circumstance. In "The Rubria Ghost" it is the ill-assorted wedding of youth and decrepitude, in "An Old-Time Episode in Tasmania" the distortions produced by the penal system, which create the drama of the situation. Also the tales afford collectively a gallery of personae in the grip of an engrossing idea or *idée fixe*. These range from the philanthropic folly of Mr Boundy through to the potentially sinister ruling passions of the Cynic and Sir Matthew Bogg. Sometimes this is treated in a humorous key, as with the English artist's obsessive but ultimately harmless search for sin and evil in the midst of Tasmania's natural beauty. More often than not, however, it threatens to transform the ostensibly rational creature, man, into a monster guilty of cruelty, bloodshed, or deep and unpardonable betrayal. Yet in the course of the particular tale, these extremes of sentiment or personality, which propel the plot unfolding, are usually modified and in some cases corrected, lending the stories an admonitory or even moral dimension, and making them not static vignettes but life-studies in individual potential.

Informing these portraits are recurring and universal concerns. Most commonly, Tasma is preoccupied with the dictates of the heart and all that impedes or complicates them. Its impulses and needs are shown to be fundamental. Her protagonists in the grip of an overwhelming and warping idea may, for a time at least, suppress them, but they inevitably reassert themselves with devastating force. Mr Paton, baulked in his passion, becomes one of those "who foremost shall be damn'd to [penal] Fame"; while the revelation of repressed and forgotten human sentiments frequently comes too late. The Cynic is compelled to enact willingly the self-immolation which, unwittingly, has constituted a major part of his life, just as Bogg's physical chastisement of his boundary rider is the logical and tragic climax to a lifetime of brutal deeds, which have severed him from affection and common humanity. Those who worship Mammon, mechanical theories and an exclusively material existence are made to pay for their denial of the spiritual and intangible emotions. But this does not reduce the tales to a fictionalised ledger of debits and credits, completed by last minute acts of redress. Tasma's appreciation of the mystery of evil impulse and the complexities of personality guaranteed against that, as did her preoccupation with the distorting effect of fixed ideas or, as she puts it in Richard's case, an "unfortunate mental crank".

Nonetheless, her firsthand knowledge of colonial conditions contributed not only an exotic, reader-enticing backdrop, it also shaped her understanding of specific characters and situations. The central encounter of 'Monsieur Caloche' dramatises, in part, what local writers had long lamented: the dire consequences for a young country in which all energies were directed towards meeting immediate material demands. Sir Matthew Bogg epitomises this concentration on physical fact, just as his bullying bumptiousness is a direct product of the kind of onesided personality which could thrive unchecked when intellectual culture, as exemplified by an "homme de lettres", counted for little. Moreover, Tasma's target here is not great wealth as such. For as she comments discriminatingly, Bogg "was a self-made man, in the sense that money makes the man, and that he had made the money before it could by any possibility make him." That is, implicitly the author allows that inherited or early acquired riches may have an enlarging and civilising effect. If gained only after formative years of toil, however, they are likely to provide the means of projecting the original man, complete with all his unimproved traits. Similarly, "How a Claim was Nearly Jumped in Gum-tree Gully" takes an archetypal pioneer situation, and uses it not to glorify national types, but to provide a general exploration of human fallibility, and of our potential to rise above this. Given our ungovernable susceptibilities and the lure of self-interest, sustainable human bonds are shown to depend on the preservation of modest ideals and basic codes of behaviour, in keeping with a premise recast variously in other tales that "It is the idea which governs—not the fact."

Perhaps her most important commentary on local characteristics, and certainly her most neglected Australian case study, is Mr Boundy in "A Philanthropist's Experiment". Occasional references to such great but foolish idealists as Cervantes' Don Quixote and Voltaire's Pangloss invite us to see him as an austral variant on the timeless theme of the incompatibility of generous impulse with the imperfect nature of creation. Yet his background, specific ideas and response to Europe make him also a prototypal, and in some ways unsurpassed, depiction of the Australian abroad. Naïve and relatively inexperienced in the complexities of human nature despite his age and position, Boundy's conception of our vital requirements is essentially bounded by physical needs. Hence, although he finds himself abased before "the marvels of the old world", he exhibits "the self-adjusting spirit of a naturalised Australian", which prides itself on the ready availability of creature comforts in the antipodes. Yet their adequacy is called into question by the reaction of the French expatriates, which suggests a longing for more than abundant food, shelter, and clean air. Admittedly, to a society that still allows its mental horizons to be circumscribed by apprehension for its young, the Parisian mother's 'unnatural' desertion of her child may seem to deprive her action of any critical force. But Tasma, through the depiction of the upstart pretensions of Burrumberie's Main Street, and through her summary verdict that life there was synonymous with "infinite stagnation", more than balances the scale. She, after all, knew firsthand the shortfalls imposed by life in a "decayed mining town" in Victoria. And she would have recognised parallels between the Parisian's final action and the choice faced intermittently by the Huybers' children and their impulsive mother, Catherine, who repeatedly decided to give up southern well-being in favour of questionable European conditions, to the probable consternation of their Australian contemporaries.

Finally, an introduction to Tasma's shorter fiction would not be complete without some reference to her depiction of female protagonists. Here again her range of characters, and her understanding of motivation and its well-springs, are impressive. The spheres of action of most of her heroines, of course, fall within the familiar roles admissible for the Victorian lady. Woman is a caring, nurturing figure, capable of inspiring heroic and ideal deeds, and of causing changes in even the commercially hardened, male breast. The two stories with Tasmanian settings, for instance, provide complementary accounts of female influence. Each demonstrates how the passion she generates can touch a mind unbalanced through over-exposure to human evil and abuses: in one case redeeming it to an appreciation of love, humankind and benevolent nature, in the other plunging it to utter damnation. Tasma's women, however, are no mere paragons, but are portrayed complexly with independent strengths and failings. Self-interest, though limited in its expression to more personal and domestic domains, is shown to be a vital motive, which makes personae like Mrs Dave and Freda James credibly human in their reactions to changing circumstances, rather than unrealistic models of propriety. As "His Modern Godiva" demonstrates, men are inclined to make a fetishistic projection of woman: a portrait fashioned according to received stereotypes and a possession to be guarded jealously. Yet in spite of concerted pressures, this particular heroine remains elusively individual, superior in reason to irrational man, and capable of throwing off constraining roles to the complete discomfiture of a would-be master who insists on the need for self-sacrifice and blind obedience.

Despite the critical gaze turned on the foibles of both sexes, there is never any doubt as to where the author's ultimate sympathies lie. For the stories, read as a group rather than in isolation, exhibit a full awareness of the circumscribed opportunities confronting womankind. It is the men who travel and grapple with external destiny, or who have clearly prescribed paths which lead to artistic careers. The women wait, serve as models, or try as best they can through their limited means to gain a share of life's plenty. Certainly the male victimiser often finds himself the unexpected victim. But at least he is responsible for his own situation, whereas Tasma's heroines are often latterday versions of Andromeda, chained to a hard fate dictated by patriarchal society, and uncertain whether their deliverer will prove to be a Perseus or a devouring monster. Beauty remains at once their pitiful weapon and their potential scourge. Its over-valuation can lead to prostitution in wedlock, or to Henriette Caloche's self-condemnation. Bereft of it, she becomes the female equivalent of the young male heir, whose lost fortune precipitates a voyage to the colonies. Her lot, however, is hopeless, because her sex precluded her from employment in the realms where wealth was to be accumulated, while with the loss of beauty she was debarred from the conventional forms of female advancement. There are, Tasma suggests, other and more important qualities associated with woman, but society's failure to appreciate their true worth costs all dear, as exemplified by Sir Matthew and "Monsieur Caloche".

Overall, then, the tales are rich in thematic resonances, acute discriminations and memorable character studies: all of which contribute to an assured command of the short story form. This was already recognised by reviewers and readers of the time. Tasma's journal records contemporary praise and not unjustified comparisons drawn between her works and those of another master of the genre, Guy de Maupassant. It also notes that the *Athenaeum* found the reprinted stories of 1890 "morbid and inconclusive". And certainly the reader who expects to find here slavish conformity to the conventions of romance will be disappointed. Tasma was too realistic and too touched by personal misfortune for that. To stock situations she brought a cultured and mature mind, capable of dispassionately drawing out the comic as well as the tragic repercussions of a relationship, and of providing penetrating analysis of human nature. This, perhaps more than anything else, lends her tales and individual scenes from longer works their enduring power, and this capacity remained with her throughout her twenty-year-long writing career. Though publishing and critical fashions led to the neglect of these works until recently, brought together now in this edition they attest to a distinctive, personal response to the conventions and themes of much late nineteenth-century fiction, and they should help us to understand why, in her day, readers believed that Tasma was entitled to claim no mean place in Australian literary culture.

MICHAEL ACKLAND
Melbourne, 1993

TEXTUAL NOTE

My special thanks are due to Mr Richard Overell, Rare Books Librarian, Monash University, for his unfailing and generous assistance, and for having made available a copy of *A Sydney Sovereign and Other Tales* (London: Truebner, 1890), for reproduction here. The other stories reprinted are drawn from their original sources, cited in the Introduction. Unless otherwise indicated, all texts are reproduced in their entirety, with only minor alterations made, either to correct rare proofreading oversights in the original, or in conformity to present house style.

WHAT AN ARTIST DISCOVERED IN TASMANIA

*Wanted, the Most Hardened Criminal on the Face of the
Earth! One whose career of depravity was entered upon
in infancy preferred. Apply RICHARD REYNOLDS SMITH,
Joshua House, Park Road, St. John's Wood.*

The reason which prevented this advertisement from figuring
in the *Times*, was an objection made to it by the artist's
sister, a young woman of sound common sense views, who
had more than once interposed when his aesthetic bias
threatened to carry him beyond bounds.

"Don't you think, Richard," she said—there was never
any blustering remonstrance, by-the-by, in her objections,
for artists resent being dictated to just as much as men you
may meet with every day—"Don't you think, Richard, it's
a little unlikely that the most hardened criminal in the world
would be in the habit of reading the *Times*? What if he
were in gaol, for instance, in the condemned cell! Besides,
when I come to think of it, I don't see why he should be
in England at all. It isn't very flattering to England to make
up your mind that you can't find the worst man in the
world anywhere out of it—is it?"

The artist's little sister couched her objections, as you see,
in the mildest of suggestions; but they were nevertheless replete
with the wisdom of the serpent. The letter of them would
seem to be sisterly anxiety that Richard should find just
such a monster as he wanted; the spirit of them was feminine
terror lest the cosy little St. John's Wood villa should be
invaded by a Bill Sykes,[1] with two clammy locks of sticky
dark hair gummed against the cheek-bones, a fur cap, and
a bludgeon, the *fac-simile*, in fact, of such a villain as she
had seen in the wood-cuts in the London *Punch*. But you

1

would never have supposed, to hear her considering the affair in a placid, business-like voice, that she had been shaking all over with terror from the time that Richard read his advertisement aloud, and that it was nothing but her dread of urging on his criminal quest—for he was always in a particular hurry to do anything he had been thwarted in— that made her desist from imploring him to abandon his idea. He would leave, as she knew, no slum in London unexplored, if once she hinted at the undesirability of inviting a thief or a murderer to the house, upon such trivial grounds as the family crested spoons, or the family brains. He had a faith in his own mesmeric power that had endured through a somewhat undignified retreat before an unappreciative bull, and an equally ignominious flight from an insane woman, who had threatened to scratch his face for staring at her. It would come to the front again with undoubting alacrity, should there be question of a murderer's pranks in his studio. At the same time, his sister would willingly spare him such a call upon his psychological powers. It took it "out of him," as he confessed, after the episode of the bull; and considering that he was backing over ploughed ground at the rate of a mile in twelve minutes, it is hardly to be wondered at if it did.

"So, Richard," she said again, "*do* consider a little, dear, before you put in that advertisement! Perhaps a counterfeit villain might come" (how devoutly she wished he would)— "the *very* worst is certain to be in gaol; and then, as I said before, why *England* of all countries in the world?"

"With reference to your first surmise, Polly," said Richard, sententiously—and I must allow that an affectation of authority became him very well, so long as he abstained from drawing upon it mesmerically—"As England knows nothing of her greatest men, I believe she knows nothing of her greatest criminals. The first are not always on a pedestal, nor the second in gaol." Richard, I must whisper in your ear, was a rejected aspirant for academical honours. "And as for your second objection, it is not unflattering, but flattering to England, to look for the completest type of any form of being—whether angelic or monstrous—within her boundaries. The extreme of good argues the extreme of ill. The worst of it is," he added, dropping suddenly from Richard the sage to Richard the confiding, "I don't know where the deuce to find my extreme of ill. There isn't a villain I've pitched upon yet who hasn't some miserable flaw in the way of a redeeming point."

"It's very discouraging," said Polly.

"Discouraging! it's simply disgusting—that's all! I'm so irritated with the half-and-half, milk-and-water specimens of depravity I drop across—I could give them a dose of vermin-killer all round. What I want is a creature like the father of the Cenci—"

"I know!" interposed Polly; "a man with a hat and plume, a scowl, a long cloak, and his left elbow always in the air."

"Not at all," said Richard, eyeing her with severe suspicion; "a creature—either man or woman—whose every breath is a blasphemous protest against the author of his being; who, feeling that he owes a grudge to everything which reminds him of his hateful existence, wreaks his spite on all around him—who would torture for the sake of torturing alone— who would go out of his way, in fact, to deface anything that was beautiful!"

"Do you think," said Polly, doubtfully, "there *are* such people, excepting in a book of tragedies?"

"There has never been a character conceived yet," replied Richard, with a fresh assumption of authority, "that had not its existence somewhere, even if it were only in the author's brain. It is a reality for him, and when he delivers himself of it, you may be sure it becomes a reality for the few or the many whose brains are shaped like his."

"But if it hasn't any *actual* existence anywhere!" hazarded Polly.

"Pooh! it becomes a subjective truth—that's all—as most truths are. Don't worry me, Polly! Give me the atlas, my tobacco-pouch, and my pipe—you will find the pipe on my easel, and don't ask any more questions, on pain of being caricatured as the modern Pandora in the next number of *Judy*. I have an inspiration!''

Richard's inspirations demanded an inaugural smoke of at least a quarter of an hour's duration, which gives me more than time to tell you all I know of him.

He was an artist, perhaps, more in sentiment than in execution. Those allusions, at least, to the overlooking of her greatest men by England, and to the potentiality, in however limited a degree, of every outcome in a creative mind, were so many protests against the apathy with which his works had been received. Yet, as artist in sentiment only, what fuller possession he enjoyed of nature's sources of delight than the thousands and thousands whose interest in the changing seasons hinges upon the drawing-room grate. It is the fashion to smile at all art that has not received the recognition of a master's approval, or a Royal glance. After which, sheep-like, we huddle in front of the masterpiece we might have blinked at before. Yet neither our scorn nor our praise can take from the one most enviable privilege of the humblest of amateur artists. The privilege, I mean, of retaining the impress made upon the mind by all that is most beautiful in the world outside of us, until in them it grows to life again, tinctured with shades of their own predominant qualities, and so becomes a bit of nature recreated by a human soul. Albeit, following the Platonic theory, that our modes of expression are but symbols, more or less irregular, of one perfect type, the mind-evolved creation may be as much less complete than its model, as are our own groping conceptions of truth compared with the Infinite Exemplar.

But this is wandering from Richard, whose foibles I am going to describe to you. Not in an uncharitable sense. There are foibles so intimately connected with the preponderance of certain fine qualities, such as over-exaltation or enthusiasm, that we love the people who possess them, knowing that an overstepping of limits of any sort must

4

cast some little shade. Polly did not love Richard a bit the less, because he made her wear sandals in his studio, and drew down a martyrdom of chilblains upon her nineteenth-century toes, during the winter months. She had lived upon a diet of carrots, milk, and potatoes for a month to please him. I think there was nothing she would not have done short of introducing that typical murderer into his studio to prove her devotion. But it weighed upon her that he should so invariably prove himself such a Frankenstein in art.[2] His monster lurked somewhere in all his creations, whether the subject were a blossoming apple-orchard on a breezy spring-day, or a mad-house in flames. And the incongruity of it was, that Richard was such a fresh-complexioned young man, with such an unassailable digestion, and such undeniably rosy cheeks, when he allowed his whiskers to be docked. He had established a kin-ship, through a somewhat questionable source, with the great Sir Joshua,[3] which Polly never thought of disputing, believing that had Sir Joshua been alive, the honour would have been all on his side.

And now—what was Richard going to do with the atlas? Polly watched him from behind the lid of her little work-table, where she was turning over despairingly his mutilated socks, gashed right and left to allow of the requisite artistic development of the second toe. He had opened it at the index—good! He was looking for a country that might be prolific of villains? No; he had turned to the second page, headed England and her possessions. Now he had shut his eyes, and was slowly, slowly puffing at his pipe. He was describing circles in the air with his forefinger over the page. Now he was bringing down his finger with a sweep. He had fastened upon a word without once opening his eyes. Polly held her breath. He solemnly opened his eyes, and directed them to the word thus caught by his finger-tip. Then turning round, he said—just as coolly, mind you, as if he had been talking of taking a trip to Scarborough—

"Polly, you must pack my trunks again. I'm going to—

to"—he looked at the word a second time—"I am going to Tasmania next week."

"Tasmania! Where's that?" cried Polly.

Kind Tasmanians—whose blossom-garlanded isle is the original Eden of the Anthropophagi; whose aromatous breezes greet the pallid stranger, and efface from his recollection the haunting odours of Yarra bank noisomeness—do not stigmatise Polly as an imbecile for her ignorance. She had been through a course of school geography, and had mastered, you may be sure, the latitude and longitude of Hobart Town, just as she had mastered the latitude and longitude of Acapulca; but somehow the whereabouts of Tasmania had escaped her.

"I know it's a long way off, Richard!" she said.

"A very long way off," replied Richard, furtively glancing at the map before he ventured to commit himself. "A ve—ry long—way—off, Polly."

"How long?" said Polly, anxiously.

"As long as the topsy-turvy side of the world," said Richard, knowingly, now that he had found the map of the group of English colonies. "It's in New Zealand— Australia, I mean. That's to say, it's just escaped being in Australia! It's a sort of Antipodal Isle of Wight, I should say, Polly."

"Oh dear!" said Polly, mournfully; "it must be part of Botany Bay!"

"Botany Bay!" cried Richard. "No! but see what it says. Transportation ceased in 1853. My inspiration, Polly! I knew it could not lead me astray. The arch-villain, whoever he may be, has been transported to Tasmania. Get me T in the Geographical Encyclopædia, Polly, and set to packing my things to-night, and don't whimper; there's a good girl. I'll bring you back the most hardened criminal on the face of the earth—life-size, and a whole museum full of cannibal curiosities; that I promise you!"

Whoever is inclined to follow Richard in quest of his monster, must come with me to Tasmania, a little before

Christmas time in the year 1870. I can promise him that the gardens will be redolent of the perfumes of roses and strawberries; the summer fruits painted with faint pink streaks, on a back-ground of transparent green; the hedge-rows along the Risdon Road rampant with scented life. Richard's artist eyes and nostrils might have revelled in the new sensation. He had left all his yule-log and holly associations behind, wreathed round by the cold grey mist of an English mid-winter. It seemed more consonant with the general jubilation of good church-goers in Christmas week that the earth should sound her pæans at the same time, instead of remaining inert under her winding-sheet of snow. It seemed to him, that for the first time nature herself acquiesced in the triumph of man. And I must add, that it seemed like black ingratitude to look for "the worm, the canker, and the grief," when there was nothing to do but to breathe in bliss along the mountain path, and undergo initiation into mountain arcana from maidens that might have peopled Arcady.

But all the blame must be laid upon Richard's unfortunate mental crank. That he grew more and more florid, did not in the least prevent him from growing more and more sombre every day. With a gloom, in fact, so pronounced, that the mothers of the afore-mentioned Arcadian maidens began to inquire into his prospects. A suicidally disposed son-in-law, possessed of entailed house property in England, not proving always an unmixed evil, from a maternal point of view.

Polly, at home in the little St. John's Wood villa, knew all about it, but then Richard had left her behind, unwilling to expose her to the chances of being captured for her plumpness by an aboriginal chief in Tasmania. She knew that when Richard was the prey of what is well called by the French an "*idée fixe*," he must needs deliver himself of it on canvas, or carry about its corroding effect on his face. And she knew that ever since their last trip to Paris, just before the war, he had surrendered himself to the idea that was holding him in thrall. That artists have these

7

crochets, is perhaps the reason why the intensity of some of their productions affects us through so many generations. And that an allegorical representation of a very ugly passion should haunt Richard so enduringly must serve as my apology for bringing him before you as an artist whose story is worth telling.

For it was nothing more than a face in that terrible group of Furies, whose malign eyes scowl at us from the carvings on the triumphal arch, that had inspired Richard with this idea. He did not want its exact counterpart for the picture that was to bring a stolid world to Polly's way of thinking, but he wanted something as mighty as its withering power—something that, regarding you with Medusa-like eyes, would hold you transfixed in a nightmare of horror. (I am sure that conception of the Gorgon must have originated with the first poet who was afflicted by indigestion among the ancients.) A something that ever after would throw its chill shade upon the most light-flecked landscape, making its victims loth to live and afraid to die. There was his idea— and I, for one, grieve that a notion so inappropriate to thirty years of healthy life, and eleven stone of unimpaired bone and muscle, should have been allowed to take possession of him. But he humoured it, I am afraid—a sure preliminary to succumbing, whether to individual or to idea that may attack you.

As humouring it after a perfectly insane fashion, I can assure you that when he was taken for the first time to an ideal brewery at the foot of the mountain, whence, if you look seaward, across a variegated crescent of descending houses and leafy gardens, a triangular-shaped stretch of the most brilliant blue gleams in the distance, like a monster turquoise: or, if you look mountainward, the calm majesty of the dark mass towering above, confronts you, with its patches of soft shade reaching away from the foot of a fluted precipice; or, if you take cognizance of what is immediately about you, a delicious aroma of garden scents, and pure fresh exhalations, and malt whose infusion makes the Cascade ale the poetry of liquors—assail your mollified senses; I can assure you that after paying the tribute of an artist, by taking off his hat to the mountain, and of an Englishman by drawing a long breath of contentment after his first draught of the beer, he turned round to inquire whether there was not an old factory somewhere in the neighbourhood. He was incorrigible, you see. It was just the same when he was taken to New Norfolk—a place about whose rock-lined, ever green-clothed river banks, even travellers from the Rhine are given to romancing. When his friends were assuring him (hypothetically, of course, in those days) that it would become one of the salmon fisheries of the world, he was pondering on the possibility of finding a good repulsive model in the asylum. That crime, madness, and old age should figure in his picture, was Richard's cheerful aim. Of crime and madness he would make the first the progenitor of the other, seeing that unrestrained wickedness has in all times developed insanity. No! he would make the last the parent of the first, as was consistent with a sounder philosophy. Stay! he would make each produce the other— but that would be painting a paradox. It was as perplexing as the hypothesis that evolves the world from an egg, and requires you to say whether the egg came first or the hen that laid it. It was as embarrassing as the story of the snakes that swallowed each other. Richard must leave this knotty question unsolved. He had been shown, finally, a point of view with which he was enraptured. Not, I am bound to admit, because it offered a profile view of the mountain, bringing into prominence the accidents that, seen from the New Town side, lend it such an enchanting irregularity; nor yet because the scene might have recalled the most picturesque of English villages under a higher, clearer sky. Only because, on a knoll girt in by native trees, interspersed with alien elms and willows, stood a building that would have given a Turk the horrors. From its clean, bare corridor and windows, the oldest of old women, in every stage of decrepit, pathetic, grotesque old age, look forth. They appear to mouth at a world that is perpetually renewed, while they cannot make good the loss of a tooth, or a failing sense. Such as have any sensation left are snappish. The oldest of all are the merriest, mumbling with idiotic satisfaction, when they warm themselves like vegetables in the sunshine. That Richard regarded this refuge as his "harem", and the Eumenides that peopled it as so many Houris, must have been the rational conclusion of those who saw how he gloated in his discovery. Gradually, one form of the blight that rests upon poor humanity took dreadful distinctness under his brush. And my artist, like all enthusiasts who prostrate themselves before the embodiment of a conception that has harassed them, could have embraced the hag who had served as his model. *Could* have! I am careful to put it in this way, lest any one should suppose he was so lost to decency as to do it. And now, heralded in by a sunrise that turned the mountain to a bulky heap of dusky red, came Christmas Day, an enforced landmark in our outer lives. Though, save for the paupers who connect it with pudding, and the children who connect it with a sock-full of treasures, it is seldom a land-mark in our inner lives. These—as every one knows—are dependent upon the birth of a new emotion; of a sensation hitherto unimagined; of some chance influence all unforeseen an hour before, for the impressions that mark off their epochs. Yet, as his first experience of a Christmas Day fragrant with roses and strawberries, there was a novelty about this one which might well serve to imprint it everlastingly upon Richard's recollection. That anything more potent than roses or strawberries should help to give it an eternal fixity, he never dreamed of suspecting, as he stood looking out of the window of his lodgings in Hampden Road, his eyes resting upon the smoothly shining waters of the harbour; his thoughts reverting to the little St. John's Wood villa far away. Polly, he was convinced, must be thinking of him that morning; he could not allow so prosaic a consideration as the fact that Polly was probably sound asleep to interfere with his fancies. But would she be careful not to desecrate his studio with those monstrous appendages called carpet slippers, that both fraternally and aesthetically he abhorred?

The severity that Richard's face assumed, as he pictured the sandals lying discarded in the corner of his studio, might have carried a warrant of the hopelessness of their pursuit to any of those far-seeing matrons, whose designs I discovered to you ere-while. It is not with reference to qualities only, but to states of feeling, that the one is negatived by the other. Hence, wiles that would have told upon even worldlier and less artless natures than Richard's, might have been all unheeded by a mind divided between the pursuit of picturesque criminality, and misgivings occasioned by the vision of a little sister, with flat-soled carpet slippers, a size too big for her; or the wiles, perhaps, would have failed from lack of comprehension of Richard's attackable point. He was under the influence of the dominant idea that allies genius with insanity, and snares that in no wise caught this idea in their meshes were found to capture—nothing!

But a dominant idea may co-exist with much surface suavity and apparent interest in matters that are inexpressibly boring, as would have been denied by nobody who was witness to the opening of Richard's Christmas Day. Polly would have looked admiringly at his new morning suit of brown, with the faintest dash of orange, and his tourist felt hat, with a brim that turned up with a kind of intuition that it was covering the crisp curls of an artist's head; only, as there was no sisterly incense—and I have already hinted that to all other incense he was as yet indifferent—to confirm his conviction that he was a fine-looking fellow, Richard contented himself with one placidly approving glance at his full length figure in the cheval-glass, and went whither he was bound.

Have I represented him as given over to one ruling and absorbing desire; one powerful craving that, for all its potency to strip the very fairest coverings from external forms, he was yet so far gone as to cherish? If I have so represented him, you will not see any inconsistency in the manner of his disposal of the sunny Tasmanian Christmas Day. While some went to hear the Bishop, and others to read "sermons in stones" on that grand tract of desolation which crowns the summit of Mount Wellington, Richard stole away to the wharf, and found his way on board a little cutter bound for Port Arthur. It was through official good-will that he had been granted the favour of a passage, a favour that his importunities only had procured him. Port Arthur had been drawing him thitherward ever since he had heard how the place was occupied—drawing him, not through its magnificent mating of rock and surf; not through its isolation; not through any attraction save its pariah population, which left open a possibility that somewhere among the yellow-jacketed convicts might be found to lurk the greatest criminal on the face of the earth. For the fact that Richard had unfortunately found his ideal of old age, gave a hopeless stability to his preconceived idea of his criminal. It is well that Polly, who would have walked down Piccadilly in the sandals, to have him back again, was devoid of second-sighted discrimination. There was a dogged resolution about his expression that augured ill for his return until his object should be achieved. I am not sure that, seeing him thus, Polly would not have gone trembling up to the Jack Ketch in power at the time, and said—"Oh, please, Mr. Ketch,[4] would you spare me your very worst murderer for an hour or two before you hang him? I want my brother back *so* much!"

To any of those perplexed antiquarians who may have racked their brains to determine the whereabouts of Cain's abode—vaguely, and if it were not inconsistent with Scriptural dignity—rather funnily alluded to in the Pentateuch as the "Land of Nod"—I would recommend a visit to Port Arthur. Whether from the association that has gathered round it, or from a natural exclusiveness breathed in its rocky boundary, it seems to scowl in its solitude like an outcast from the mainland. The first murderer might have bared his branded forehead to the salt breezes that blow across it, and so infused into its atmosphere a foretaste of the presence of his descendants. Human influences always affect us so much more than natural ones. The salt breezes may blow across Port Arthur at the present time, untainted by convict breath, yet I question whether the echo of the clanking chain, and the reprobate's curse, will not sound above the "swish" of the tide and the rustling of the fruit trees for many a generation to come.

But I am forgetting myself. To connect Christmas-tide with crime is clearly unpardonable. Even Richard's morbid cravings do not incline me to look leniently upon the solecism of linking depravity with Divinity. I refer any one for whom the annals of a criminal life may have a fascination to "His Natural Life," upon which he may sup "full with horrors"; albeit the story is anything but a dismal treatise.

Richard was reading it, as it came out in numbers, at the time of his visit to Tasmania. The "giant" approached closely to his ideal type of the form that a body might assume, invested with such tendencies as he had described to Polly. If the mania for statistics had only averaged criminal heights and weights, and affixed thereto a certain order of crime, he could have specified the number of feet and inches his criminal must measure in his boots. As it was, he only felt that the more Miltonic in its proportions the better, as more closely allied with the ancient mythological conception, and the present practical conception of evil in a humanized form.

The nature of Richard's credentials, from the eligibility of which even the flavour of Bohemianism that lurked in his outer man had not detracted one whit, procured him the entrée into the very selectest of prison society. It would have seemed that, in the *embarras de richesses* before him, there was nothing but to pitch upon "his one man picked out of ten thousand."

But alack!

The best laid schemes o' mice and men
Gang aft agley!

In the course of its circulation round that sun-caressed, crime-stained little world, the rumour that there was a great artist who had authority from the Home Government—a rumour which Richard, I must confess, did not publicly refute—to cite before him the "most hardened criminal on the face of the earth," reached other ears than the ears of those impersonal beings known as Heads of Departments. Now, that the ears in question were feminine ears, will be inferred by the least discriminating of readers, when I attest the greed with which they drank in all the details bearing upon the mysterious mission of the artist. They had further, in addition to the foregoing essential quality, the purely accidental one of being affixed to the most charming head ever seen out of a picture by Greuze. Though, at the precise period of my story, this head laboured under the disadvantage of being closely cropped all round, which resulted in giving its owner the air of a cherub who was doing a sentence. I hasten to explain that it was not vice but fever that led to this suggestive docking of her yellow curls. And, moreover, that had she not been in the idle stage following upon fever, a stage whose attendant pallor, by-the-by, was infinitely becoming to the cherubic cast of her face, I do not think she would have conceived that daring scheme with reference to Richard's design, which I must reluctantly unfold to you. Good Dr. Watts, in crediting his personal Devil with such alacrity in the way of finding "bad jobs" for idle hands, might have told us how equally prompt he proves himself in advancing suggestions to an idle woman's brain. If Eve had only had a Paradisiacal household to look after, do you think he could have inveigled her into a discussion about the qualities of an apple that she could not even put into a celestial dumpling? I am sure it was from sheer mental vacuity that she and Adam each took a bite, just as I am sure that if my little Port Arthur heroine had had any profounder occupation than the watching of the convict gangs file past

14

the garden, the wily Devil would never have found any scope in her brain for putting his propositions into form.

It all began in this way. She was romantic—for romantic, read largely endowed with the organ of Ideality—and rejoicing, or rather repining, under the homely baptismal name of Jane, and the unhappily sequential surname of Jones, was addicted to tracing upon the sand, in large characters, "Janet Vere" or "Janet Cholmondley". Being absorbed in this characteristic pastime one day, Richard passed her by—given up, as was now his wont, to his dominant idea. Jane confessed afterwards to her cousin and confidante, Susan, who stood in the same useful relation to her that Racine's confidantes bear to his queenly heroines, "that she had watched the great artist as he walked with his head down until he was out of sight." Furthermore, that she hoped she might be forgiven for saying such a wicked thing, but really if she could only be the most hardened criminal on the face of the earth for just a week or two—and sometimes, she must confess, she felt wicked enough to go to any lengths—she thought she would be very, very happy. And Susan dear, who knew her so well, would keep her secret as long as both of them lived. Wouldn't she? Susan dear was quite sure that the secret should die with her. Whereupon Jane felt emboldened to detail the emotions that Richard's beautiful colour had aroused. The prisoners as a rule were pasty-faced, and Susan's father, who was a warder, had a skin in which a keen observer saw traces of a vinous habit of body. Hence the description of Richard's cheeks touched a powerful chord of sympathetic interest. Susan was willing to abet her dearest Jane in any plan that might lead to a nearer examination of them. What could such willingness result in, save the concoction by these two feminine heads of a scheme of unparalleled daring? None but an artist who was going through a phase of almost total mental ablepsy, consequent upon his dominant idea, could have been its victim for an instant. In its audacious defiance of all possible rules and regulations, it might have formed the ground-work of the plot of an opera bouffe by Offenbach! I hesitate to disclose it out of pure consideration for Richard, whom, in spite of his floridity and his follies, I should regret to render ridiculous.

But a conscionable chronicler should know no scruples. It is on record, then, that the same evening, the evening of Boxing Day, Richard was accosted in the dusk—that short-lived gloaming of Austral latitudes—by a young man who, at first sight, recalled a pantomime policeman; and who, speaking in a voice of preternatural gruffness, as was consistent with his pantomimic demeanour, explained to him that the very next day, at noon, in the summer-house of warder Jones's garden, he might have an audience of "the most hardened criminal on the face of the earth." The following conditions must, however, be enforced:—

Condition No. 1.—The criminal would serve as model for one hour only.

Condition No. 2.—The artist, upon no pretext whatever, was to exchange any conversation with the criminal. He might, however, give him directions as to the pose he was to assume.

Condition No. 3.—The policeman who gave the artist this information was to guard the door of the summer-house with a loaded revolver, to be used at discretion should the stringent regulations be broken.

The readiness with which the artist acquiesced in the foregoing absurd conditions must be looked upon as painful evidence of the extent to which he had succumbed to his idea. We know the lunatic will give ear to the wildest proposition touching upon the notion which preys on his brain. In his justifiable exultation, Richard failed to notice the searching glance directed by the policeman at his cheeks. He continued his walk, with the sensations of an ecstatic who has received a forewarning of a beatific vision—bestowing scant attention upon the purple glow that gathered with the darkness upon the far-reaching sea, or upon the pale horizon, that seemed to climb away from the slate-coloured expanse and melt into heavenly tones of delicate amber and green. What contrasted harmonies of sea and sky compared with the

convict's scowl that was to satisfy his soul's thirst on the
morrow?

Sleepless hours, dragging in their wake tales of old incanta-
tions, brought Richard his morrow. But would they bring him
the entire satisfaction he craved? Be a hope ever so fully
realized, is there not always a something in the conditions of
its realization that we would fain order differently? Now, the
summer-house was the condition in the fulfilment of
Richard's desire that he felt to be inappropriate and superfluous. So overlaid with a tangle of scarlet passion-flower,
starred with white jasmine of almond-like scent, and vine-
leaves fluttering against caressing tendrils, that it recalled the
arbour where Paris passed in review the charms of competing
goddesses. He sate himself down, resenting the inroad of the
odours from the garden without. The minas and parrots were
squeaking with delight; the magpies sounded a note, born of
freedom in the wilds, that was like an inspired taunting of
the human captives. Richard adjusted his pencil of charcoal,
and his cardboard, exulting in the prospect of branding its
unmeaning surface with the embodiment of his idea, yet,
withal, half repining because the clamorous rejoicing of birds
and insects seemed to mock at the gloom that his prepared-
ness for the reception of his ideal should plainly have brought
with it. He waited, with his ears closed against the singing
and the chirping, until a shadow fell from the doorway across
the table. Then Richard looked up.

The most hardened criminal on the face of the earth stood
before him—with limpid eyes, that, by reason of their colour,
might never have been directed other than heavenward. The
black convict cap, rising to a hideous peak in the middle,
covered a small head of docked yellow hair, that already began
to assume rings of floss-like texture round the transparent
temples. Anything more spotlessly fair and smooth than the
skin of this most hardened criminal, or more warmly red than
his childish-looking, innocent mouth, I defy you to have

found. The prison uniform, indicating the depth of his depravity by a yellowness as complete as was ever presented by a young chicken, could not take from his fairness. It came out even in his delicate hands—in which a row of dimples did duty for knuckles; in his slender wrists, so much too small for their manacles that the narrow escape he had of letting them slip to the ground almost made this hardened criminal laugh.

Do you suppose Richard was so wholly and solely an artist as to have nothing of an every-day man's impulses left within him? I must say to his credit, that, after the first prodigious start of surprise, he blushed until even the pantomime policeman thought there might be limits to the dye of fresh-complexioned cheeks. If he conceived, in the first shock of astonishment, that he had encountered that lost spirit—

Who stole the livery of the Court of Heaven
To serve the Devil in,

he thought something more worthy of Polly's brother when the shock of astonishment was over. Whether, in leaving him, it startled away the main part of his morbidity, or whether the eyes of the most hardened criminal had as exorcising an effect as had David's harp upon Saul given up to doleful dumps, I have not ascertained. Something must have had an instantaneously transforming effect upon his mind to make him resolve upon the following apparently inconsistent course.

He arranged the pose of his criminal with perfect gravity, removing the prison-cap with his own hands, and so placing the yellow head that a back-ground of variegated green seemed to frame it. The light, that only dulled the uniform, appeared to gild the criminal's head until you would have said it was encircled by an aureola within a wreath. As Richard sketched, fixing his eyes intently from time to time upon the delicious picture in front of him, he wondered why, half an hour ago, the trilling on the summer-house roof had annoyed him. It thrilled him now, as chiming in with some new conception of art that had just overwhelmed him. It was quite true that, had he chosen to grovel under the dead wood in the ditch beyond, he might have unearthed long repellant snakes, or active hairy tarantulas, or centipedes that leave leprous marks in their trail. But when, between reptiles and birds, these persisted in coming into his path, and insisting upon the abandonment of the jubilation of the Southern world at Christmas time, while those hid all their loathesomeness and slime deep down out of his reach, it seemed to his later-born perceptions that there was profanity in rebelling against such an ordaining.

I am not sure that, when the pantomime policeman put his hand upon his revolver at the exact expiration of the hour, either criminal or artist entirely approved of his zeal.

"You will bring your prisoner to-morrow," Richard said to him while the yellow head was disappearing into the convict cap. "I'm afraid he's not quite wicked-looking enough," the policeman surmised, in a voice of such muffled hoarseness that the convict was observed to go through agonies of suppressed laughter.

"Too wicked-looking, if anything," said the artist, very gravely; "don't you think so?" and he held his drawing up.

The convict, with a flagrant disregard of discipline, ran in front of the policeman to see the picture first, but said nothing, being shame-faced, in her villainous garb, in presence of so idealized a conception. The policeman said—"Oh my!" in a tone of shrill delight, that was free from even a suspicion of hoarseness; but I think, from the artist's expression, the silent criticism touched him most.

For you never saw a sketch so inspired by the spirit that had dictated it. Its tendency was all in an upward direction. Earthward dragged souls—despondent eyes—looking upon it, could not have failed to grasp fresh heart, fresh courage, in view of so palpable a presentment of hope, with sublime regard directed aloft. In lieu of streaming hair, festoons of verdure, so delicate that the leaves seemed to tremble as you looked, garlanded the head. The light that pierced in a soft ray through an aperture in the knotted stalks overhead, seemed to shine directly into the eyes, and radiate therefrom with benignant, cheering influence. The rounded head of a little bird appeared in a corner of the aperture, with beak that seemed to drink the ray, and emit so vigorous a warble of promise, that you paused, as waiting for its note to reach your inner senses. It was the enfranchisement of a spirit, the acknowledgment of a something far removed from the ditch which would have been Richard's goal that morning.

The spiritual face, looking out of the foliage, was clogged, you may be sure, by no chain-weighted body. Richard indicated this to the policeman, as prefacing a request he had still to make.

"You see, those yellow clothes are incongruous. If your"— he hesitated to use the word "prisoner" in full view of the portraiture of Hope incarnate—"if my model," he said, gently, "would wear something of a white robe or wrap to-morrow, I could complete my sketch."

I think I said awhile ago that it is the soul's impressions, not the calendrical fast or feast days, that divide the life into its distinct epochs. It happened to Richard, however, that the birth of the new sentiment whence he dated the inauguration of his fuller life, was co-existent with that season wherein "the bird of dawning singeth all night long;" which led to his investing Christmas week, ever after, with an aspect it had never worn before he came to Tasmania.

But the prosaic sequel of the story—for only an ecstatic (which is another word for lunatic) can live upon a sentiment maintained at concert-pitch—may be found in the following letter from Richard, sent, I believe, by the February mail.

"DEAR POLLY,—I return in April, and shall bring you, according to my promise, the most hardened criminal on the face of the earth (picture Polly's trepidation). Have the furniture new chintzed with your usual good taste, and burn the carpet slippers.—Yours, &c., RICHARD."

But it was not because he had encountered a young woman of cherubic features, and strongly marked flirting proclivities, that Richard's life was thenceforth as roseate as his cheeks. It was because the sudden, sweet violence done to the idea he had been fostering in violation of his organization, left unhampered his naturally happy, kindly impulses. As a painter of English country loveliness, he has already made a reputation. If his wife had a pang in perceiving that Jane Smith was hardly less ineligible for the part of a heroine of romance than Jane Jones, she found much assuagement of it at the separate christenings of Michael Angelo, Raphael, and Rosa Bonheur Smith. Richard, I must add, might command any price for his pictures—but the one that no fabulous offers will induce him to sell, is a little charcoal sketch of almost celestial meaning—that never fails to lift him out of himself, and to which he declares himself indebted for that joy-inspiring tone that is the main feature of his works, and the real secret of their success.

THE RUBRIA GHOST

I wonder why, in the face of all the unexplained phenomena that are always greeting us in this generally phenomenal world of ours—an unexplained ghost should be so uniformly goaded and worried—every shred of character, even to its very existence, which seems to be a sort of aimless and unsatisfactory one at the best of times, torn from it—and itself impeached and hounded down, until, from being a sociably-inclined ghost, it takes to sulking, and remains altogether out of the way of its detractors. Though from what I can gather of the habits of ghosts, they are not gregarious at the best of times; a proof, I imagine, of their consideration for mortals—one ghost at a time being usually found sufficient company for anyone, and indeed, quite a host in itself. They are shrinking, too, and timid, requiring as many conditions in the way of darkness and antiquity, before they will favour any special locality, as a prince might require in the way of comfort and grandeur, before he could be induced to settle down in any particular neighbourhood.

Objection might certainly be taken to their good breeding, on the score of their general disregard of conventionality. In the last century, especially, we hear of pushing ghosts who thought nothing of intruding upon even the privacy of the bed-chamber, and though it must be admitted that no Russian waltzer could have glided among the furniture with less detriment to it, these ghosts lacked the essential of good manners in their reluctance to efface themselves, when they were "*de trop*". I say, "in the last century", advisedly, for what with telegraphs as a sort of forestalling of second sight, and photographs and phonographs, as a more complete reproduction of the identity of the departed, than the completest warranted ghost could pretend to—they have found, like Othello, their occupation gone. I don't know how many tables, and cabinets, and dim lights, and excited brains, and inordinate faith, it doesn't require now-a-days, to coax even the very shallowest ghost out of its stronghold. And ghosts are not good company either. I do not say this in the way of an aspersion, but because it is forced upon my mind by a recollection of the ghost of Rubria, upon which, indeed, my story hinges.

Of course it had its idiosyncrasy. We know that there are—

> *Black spirits and white,*
> *Red spirits and grey;*

and that notwithstanding that little tendency to make themselves at home, without a formal invitation, of which, as I have explained, they seem to have cured themselves latterly, ghosts have their *amour-propre* as well as more solid individuals. This general feature, vouching for their human origin, argues the possession of distinctive characteristics likewise, and enables me to affirm of the Rubria Ghost, that what I must call, for want of a better word, its "selectness", was its one predominant and most disagreeable quality. This it was which made it even poorer company than the general run of ghosts. For, as it took the mean advantage of never disclosing itself to more than one person at a time, and was quite unlike the ghost of Hamlet's father, who was not at all particular about the number of people he entertained collectively, and seems as a ghost to have been fond of a little buffoonery in a quiet way, it followed that there could be no braving it in parties, no excuse for pleasant moonlight outings, no graceful flutterings on the part of young lady visitors, no possible "*raison d'être*", such as comets and considerate ghosts have been known to supply, for mysterious and blissful wanderings among dew-besprinkled, night-invaded pathways. Perhaps the sense that in a country like Australia, as young in all that constitutes age in countries, as a fine baby in leading-strings, the genus ghost had hardly had time to develop itself, may have had something to do with the retiring disposition of the Rubria Ghost. Perhaps the evident incongruity of associating itself occasionally with anything so prosaic as the woolshed of a sheep-station, may have helped to confirm this natural bashfulness. I can only surmise, in respect of the opinions it may have held, from its own ghostly point of view. As for the facts, I am prepared to state them clearly and unwaveringly—after Burns' conception of them, indeed, as—

> *Chiels that winna ding*
> *An' daurna be disputed.*

And of all these indisputable facts, I hold none more indisputable than the fact of the Rubria Ghost. In the first place, everyone had seen it, that is to say, everyone on the station had had a private view of it within three months from the time of its first appearance, when, on a cloudy night, it actually chased the stockman from the well, a place, by the way, that his own proclivities did not lead him to patronise too extensively, as it was. The manager, indeed, fond of pungent suggestions, whether in conversation or curry, for a long time "d——d the ghost, and everyone who had seen it;" which, as the boundary rider, who had a turn for epigram remarked, "might only help to give it a sense of fellowship, as it was probably that way already." But even the manager's goodwill did not suppress the ghost.

Of course, like every other abstract fact, upon which it is impossible to get at a united judgment, the Rubria Ghost was differently translated by all the minds that had been brought into contact with it. If you had depended for a knowledge of it upon the individual impressions of the station-hands, you would have learnt that it was white, that it was black, that it was tall, that it was small, that it planted behind trees, that it skipped round stumps with a kind of diabolical prance, that it "ran at people,"—a vague and horrible accusation, putting it almost on the level of a bull—and that it was, taking it altogether, too fearful and intangible a ghost to be rightly described.

Now, as affecting Rubria, in a marketable sense, that is to say, as a station renowned for sending a fair percentage of fat sheep to the Melbourne market, I am well aware that the ghost carried no more weight than might be expected from a spirit of its substance, or rather, no substance; but as affecting it in a habitable sense, as the prospective home of a beautiful English bride, it was something of a drawback to know that quiet reflections upon the tranquillity of the moonlit plains might be disturbed by the inconsequent gambols of an ungainly ghost. Which was a catastrophe as certain to ensue sooner or later, as the impending catastrophe that is to hurl us into the sun, or freeze away all our caloric, in a few billion years. For the ghost, with a nice discrimination, hardly to be looked for from a new chum of a ghost, had chosen for its beat just such a spot as a newly-arrived home-girl might turn into her bower and weave an airy fabric in, winding it about her spirit, under shelter of the pines and ferns—to the detriment of that more solid fabric of gold and silver, she had imprisoned herself in so remorselessly. A natural footpath, fringed with tangled scrub of leathery fern, and magenta heath, and dainty eucalyptus sapling, wound itself, clean and white, through myrtle shrubs down to the very edge of the river. But before losing itself among the reed-covered banks, it halted in the midst of a natural clump of Murray pines, softly, mysteriously dark and green, where, just after sunset, fragrant peppermint odours mingled with the fresh exhalations from the river below, and the wild laughing chorus of the jackasses and magpies, like the mirth of the goblins in the Catskill mountains, seemed to mount on high in an abandonment of unrestraint, blended with the wild scents of the primeval bush. But what had all this to do with the bride? The track was a narrow one, even before threading its way in labyrinthine fashion through the heart of the clump of pines, but there was room for two beings who had "hit the mood of Love on Earth".

What carnal or spiritual reason could the most sagacious of ghosts have had for inferring that it must needs be trodden by only one, and that one "a true and honourable wife"?

If you had been at Rubria on that particular October night when the newly-married pair arrived, and had looked at bride and bridegroom, with the coldly-impartial eyes of a person who sees "studies" as a surgeon sees "subjects" in every poor palpitating piece of humanity, you would have admitted that there might be something in the foresight of the ghost. I cannot recall all those trite comparisons regarding the linking of May and December, and crabbed age and youth, and spring and winter, which so inevitably occur when there is a margin of fifty years between husband and wife. I can only marvel, as the manager did (though affirming my amazement, perhaps, less profanely), at so incongruous a mating.

Hebe's face, with the blood of six generations of milk-imbibing Devonshire ancestors crimsoning her full lips—Hebe's figure,[5] encased in a French cut robe that lent itself to every exquisite curve beneath—that was the bride. As for the bridegroom, well, "Oh! Flesh, flesh, how art thou fishified!" A palsied head, acquiescing, with senile chuckle and dribbling lips, in the closing farce that was soon to make it rigid; cold, cramped fingers, clinging to youth's firm arm; filmy, red-rimmed eyes; shaking legs, that could totter only to the grave—that was the bridegroom.

I think the most terrible thing connected with him was the pale reflection of passion that flickered in his dulled eyes every time they rested on his wife. But then there was a redundancy of youth and bloom about her, that might have reanimated the chill blood of any worn-out David. He had long ago passed that central phase in man's life when our self-love takes the pleasing form of deferring to others, as a means of securing their good-will, and had relapsed into the infant's unabashed notion of regarding self as the pivot round which the world revolves. And, notwithstanding, she appeared to cherish him! If, indeed, he had been one of those wayward infants whose *naïve* self-absorption it is so easy to pardon, instead of a doting infant of eighty, with gleams of sensuality, she could not have served him more faithfully.

The station hands were accustomed to see her lead him, on sunny mornings, to the verandah, where she would prop him up in a great arm-chair, hedge him in with hot bottles and air-cushions, inflated by her own sweet breath, and walk beneath the over-arching creepers, nodding and smiling at him as she went. If she stepped beyond an imaginary boundary that he had feebly conceived as her limit, a faint cracked voice would make itself heard—"Em-my, Mrs. Ja-son, wi-ife, come!"—The cry was in a kind of minor key, very plaintive, and out of tune; but she never allowed it to be repeated. She ran to him at once, and patted his flannel cap or stroked his cheeks, whereat he would whimper with gratification; and every day the same scenes would be repeated, until she put him to bed at dusk. Then only, after a faint sing-song snore proclaimed him to be asleep, she would cover her face with her hands, and crying, perhaps, with the Psalmist, from the bottom of her heart, "How long! O Lord! how long?" would run from the atmosphere imbued with the presence of unwholesome old age, and breathe largely of the pure air without.

And how about the chance of encountering the ghost? I think a constant sense of the pressure of some self-inflicted nightmare, such as many of us incontinently burden our lives with, is a sure shield against ghostly terrors. Is it not misery always that courts the supernatural? It seems sometimes as if only a miraculous aid could save us from the effects of our own blunders, but who that is well content with his lot would not scout miraculous aid!

Emily felt one night that the final note of that inward cry she was always sending forth against her destiny had been reached at last. Old Jason had been captious in the forenoon, and the wiles by which she had humoured him had so captivating an effect, that he seemed to be infused with a ghastly rekindling of youth's ardour. She could have fled from his fondling to the bottom of the deepest coal-pit, and felt herself less sullied by the contact of the blackening smut than by the touch of his grisly lips. He was thriving like an infant under her care. Sickened and despairing, she coaxed him to sleep, chanting to him a refrain that sounded in her ears like the dirge of her own immolated youth, and escaped—escaped, as far as her loathsome office allowed—for, as she asked herself that evening, in how much was she better than those criminals of old whose ghastly punishment it was to be chained to the body of a corpse! His cracked voice was the chain that restrained her, and reminded her of the clog at the end of it. She thought all these things as she went outside to-night. The homestead behind her was a huge vault. It was full of charnel associations. She took the path towards the river instinctively, as if the night mists rising from its bosom could purify her. She had thrown a little scarlet shawl over her head, and either this, or her dreary reflections, made her look pale in the evening light. The boundary-rider, returning to the homestead, could descry her scarlet hood, like a large robin-red-breast among the pines in the distance. These trees, too, were old and twisted, but what sheltering arms they stretched out! what moist aromatic perfumes their ancient branches seemed to exhale! Was it only Humanity that must not grow old? Remembering the old man lying asleep within the house, Emily could have found it in her heart to die like "those whom the gods love"—even now, with every youthful impulse ready to respond to the physical life around—rather than to gain old age at any cost, or with any flattering promise, though it should be an old age

> *Serene and bright,*
> *And lovely as a Lapland night.*

Were the pine-trees cognisant of her desires? Was there a heart within their thick-set trunks that beat with her own, or had the Hamadryads,[6] driven out of Greece, found shelter behind the tattered bark of the Australian gums? For as surely as she was standing in the midst of the clump of pines, with her pale

29

face flushed by the red sunbeams piercing their branches, so surely she heard her own name, "Emily,"—first in a whisper—"Emily," then louder, "Emily, Emily," and then she turned her head.

The ghost was struggling with some white head-gear, that looked suspiciously like a flannel jersey drawn over its face. A shame-faced ghost, detected at the outset, and a long-legged broad-shouldered ghost, as you would have said when the jersey was torn off, and an accusing ghost too, before whose pained handsome eyes Emily's head seemed to sink, as she stood with her back to one of the pines, and cried out "Oh, Tom! *You!*—"

"Yes," said the ghost, half making as if he would have taken her into his arms, and then suddenly remembering. "What did I say when you broke faith with me? What did I say when you drove me away?"

"That you'd haunt me always, Tom."

"And so I have, though you mayn't have seen me; and so I will. Aren't you mine? When I knew how they had desecrated you"—he waved his hand in the direction of the homestead with a gesture of repugnance—"I felt so bitter, Emily, I could have killed you and myself too. That is over now. I have suffered too much."

"Oh, Tom!"

"Not that I believe you care. It's quite enough for me to see you looking so fresh and beautiful. That's proof enough for me. May the Lord forgive me, Emily. But I'll put an end to it. If any ghost troubles you now, it won't be a flesh-and-blood one; that's all about it."

"Oh, Tom!"

She made a step forward. The ghost's nervous arms seemed to envelop her all in a minute, and she cried with her face against the ghost's shoulder as if her heart would break.

"Emily, my darling, come away from it all; come right away with me now! Don't hang on waiting for that poor old wretch to die. He's good for any number of years. It's a lie to say you're his wife. I don't care how many churches you were married in. Come, and I'll keep you like a lady. I'll slave so that you shan't do a hand's turn. Wouldn't I——."

But it is hard to say what he *would* have done. What he did do, was to kiss her over and over again, while she still cried quietly. She was thinking all the time of what was lying there in the house, at the end of her chain. The remembrance of it a moment ago had made her almost willing to die, but if, instead of dying, she should live, and live only for her lover, throwing to the winds all thought of social restrictions, all prospect of those riches which had once seemed to her worth the sacrifice of her youth, and her purity, and her womanhood? Could it be holier to toil on, waiting for a dead man's shoes, that she might see them filled by her handsome penniless sweetheart, than to retract her evil bargain, and atone? What, if the atonement should involve the loss of prospective wealth, and her own good name?

She knew that the tribunal before which good names are arraigned signified nothing here in the Wilds. And was wealth of any consequence, either? Was not the natural wealth of youth, and vigour, and beauty, the natural impulse that would have made them blend their lives into one, worth all that artificial mockery of wealth she had left behind her?

It is the same with individuals as with countries. They never know till sickness lays the one low, and famine or war devastates the other, that wealth does not mean clinking bits of metal, but something inherent, some inward springs of well-being, without which even the wealth that lay in Midas' finger-tips would be as nought. In real wealth they were as rich as the offspring of a golden age—and should she cast it all away for a delusion?

"Tom, I will come back," she whispered at last. "Wait till it is dark, wait till midnight, if you will. I *must* return now; the people will be talking. I shall come, *really*. And oh! take me away, Tom, do! I'm so tired of it all."

She was speaking straight out, as Nature bade her. I cannot say that the ghost did just what he ought to have done, and argued down these impulses. On the contrary, he pleaded even harder than Nature herself, and swore to his love that he would devote every fibre in his body, every sentiment of his soul, to her, and to her only, for ever and ever.

The boundary-rider was close as well as epigrammatic. He did not confide to anyone that evening his suspicion that "young Mrs. Jason was 'thick' with the ghost;" holding, perhaps, that "thickness" with immaterial essences was no more reprehensible on her part than on the part of the good king Numa, or anyone else who seeks ghostly countenance. Nevertheless, he watched her run back to the house by moonlight, with her little scarlet wrapper fluttering behind. I daresay he would have liked to see her when she got inside, and with her wrapper thrown down, and her beautiful lips parted, and breathing hard after her run, stood irresolute, with uplifted lamp, looking at her husband's shrivelled hand, depending from the bed wherein she had laid him. Psyche may have looked so when she approached Cupid with the lamp, her eyes full of dread at the possibility of beholding a monster.[7] For Emily, as if fascinated, drew nearer to the bed, and allowed a subdued stream of light to fall aslant her husband's face. What pathos there was in it, to be sure! What a mute protest against the old age that had made him so unlovely! The blear eyes had quite disappeared into their hollow sockets; the wisp of hair escaping from beneath his nightcap upon his creased forehead, the pale line that showed where his fallen lips (unsupported by his toothless gums) had merged into each other—all spoke of his helplessness, all appealed to the sense of pity she shared in an emotional way with the generality of women; and while she stood looking, his withered lips moved, as if he felt his dependence on her even in sleep, and articulated tremulously the cracked cry—"Em-my, Mrs. Ja-son, wi-ife, come!"

Now the gold, the prospective possession of beautiful, hateful Rubria, the sheep, the plains, sank into nothingness.

These, I can declare, had nothing to do with the impulse which made her fall upon her knees, and swear to retract her former resolve. He stood in such terrible need of her.

The thought of his looking out for her in the morning, with his poor worn-out eyes, was too sad and too cruel. Tom must hear reason!

She had burdened her life with the daily decaying life that now rested upon hers. Nature had two voices after all, or was it duty only that cried out to her now, and told her she would be a murderess if she abandoned this life that she held in her hands? She was very white when she rose from her knees. Her resolution was taken.

But old Jason had taken his resolution too. How few of us know when our day is over! I think that opportune inspiration of his expiated all his fretfulness, his exactingness, his repulsive fondling. Emily had not had time to turn away from the bed, when the change that so soon brings us all—age and youth, beauty and ugliness—to the same uncomely level, fell upon his face. He muttered in feeble choking tones his old cry,—"Em—my, Mrs. Ja—son, wi—ife, come!"—and so went.

It may be that what faint life his wife had hitherto sustained in him, had succumbed before the chill of her intended desertion. Influences are so subtle, and their range is so little understood. The fact is there. She had put him to bed, shuddering at his ghastly rejuvenescence, and now, two hours later, he was dead.

But all this is obviously very wrong and very immoral,—for of course, she married almost directly, and kept house with the ghost. But what a shocking moral! Here was a woman who had done worse than many a courtesan of ancient Rome—selling, under cover of the church, instead of fairly and openly, her virgin beauty for gold. It was a shameless sale. And when she sickened of her bargain, she would have made matters worse by flying from one sin into another. For though it may be charitable to conclude that she quite intended to keep all the vows inspired by the sight of her sleeping husband, I, for one, am inclined to think a little more pressing from the ghost would have shaken her resolutions considerably. And just in the very nick of time her husband dies, and leaves her all his property, and there is nothing—both she and the ghost being robust, and young, and prosaic—to stand in the way of their enjoying themselves for evermore.

But I have one thing to say in apology. How many of my readers have ever seen a moral properly worked out in real life? Is any one of them unable to call to mind some very worthy and obviously meritorious individual, who ought, according to the most rudimentary principles of poetical justice, to be having a good time of it, and who, instead, is having a very sorry time of it altogther? Don't they know, without being uncharitable, people without end, worldly, sharp, and pushing, whose lines have fallen in pleasant places, and who have nothing to do but to sail merrily through life with a fair wind all the time? And again, in extenuation of the immorality of the story, which, being a story, should, of course, belie real life, and have a big moral at the end of it: who can say whether anyone is happy until the end? We all know what Solon, poet, politician, and wise man—the two former definitions for the most part quite exclusive of the latter—said to the Lydian king on the subject of happiness.[8] Poor pampered Crœsus! whose very name conveys in the pronunciation of it, such a sense of richness and repletion. Was it only in vindication of the sage's warning that the gods suffered you to be brought so low? Your cry of "Solon! Solon!" will re-echo through the Ages so long as man inhabits a world of catastrophes—so long as, day after day, he learns how individual welfare is swamped by those "most disastrous chances" we can none of us foresee.

So for anyone who is outraged upon hearing that Emily married the ghost, and that she and he are now in the spring-time of their delight, I will offer this pale reflection of a moral: Who can foresee the end? Let us hope he will beat her.

ROBINA'S AWAKENING

[Taken from Chapter V, entitled "Temporary Eclipse of the Sovereign", from *A Sydney Sovereign*.

Reginald Barrington is recalled from Australia to the family estate upon the death of his elder brother, but before departing he is asked to visit in the Old World his overseer's half-sister, Robina Marl, and to give her a newly minted Sydney Sovereign. Robina, at the time, is preparing for communion under Reginald's younger brother, and a fortuitous meeting takes place between her and Reginald when she is playfully set upon by his dog. Although long bespoken for to the faithful Lucy, Reginald is instantly smitten by Robina's fresh charms. He accompanies her home to the cottage-door, pressing the sovereign into her hand, and pledging her to place the coin in the next church collection as proof that his opening transgressions have been forgiven. (ed.)]

"You must not forget our compact," he said, and he held out the yellow Sydney sovereign again. This time Robina took it without a word, and Mr. Barrington raised his hat to her in token of adieu. But, as he did so, he looked at her with an expression for which the Nemesis in the widow's cap might have visited him with even severer reprobation than for what was already on his conscience. For it was the kind of look that might have stirred the emotional nature of even a seasoned flirt. Robina had been as Eve before the Fall up to the moment of receiving it. But from the instant that a man's eyes have enabled a woman to read that she has found favour in his sight—from the instant that the revelation has brought a throb of rapture with it, and that she is moved by the sense of a power which makes her feel, for the moment, as rich as though all that Satan showed Christ from the summit of a high mountain were within her grasp—from that instant her Garden of Eden closes upon her for ever. She has tasted of a fruit whose flavour will remain within her lips to the end of time. Things will have a new meaning for her. The fair universe that she has gazed upon so innocently hitherto will begin to put on the inevitable subjective aspect that a knowledge of the secret springs which move it must induce. Robina, entering into the tiny hall of Ivy Cottage, with her fingers closed on the sovereign for the plate, her heart beating tumultuously, was no longer the same as the Robina who had left it an hour or two ago, her church service and exercise book in her hand, and thoughts that for all their metaphysical complexity might have been enshrined under cover of the church service in her brain.

She hesitated for a moment before the door of the parlour (at Ivy Cottage the dining-room, drawing-room, and work-room were all merged into a twelve-foot-square enclosure that was known as the parlour), listening to the click of the sewing-machine under her mother's active fingers. The gold felt strange and heavy against her palm. She had never possessed more than five shillings of her own, all at once, in her life. As she opened the door a grey, faded face, with inquisitorial eyes, turned itself round upon her. "You have been wasting your time, child," was all her mother's greeting, for Mrs. Marl's one rule of life was "up and doing," and time spent in meditation was time thrown away. "Mr. Barrington cannot possibly have kept you all this time. I am certain of *that*."

A Jesuit would have sworn that none other than Mr. Barrington was answerable for the delay, but Robina's new education had not, happily, carried her so far as yet. Nevertheless, she felt an unaccountable reluctance to explain the real reason of her coming in so late. She displayed her injured hat, and recounted her adventure with the dog after a somewhat confused and hurried fashion. That she should have said nothing whatever about the manner of her rescue was the strongest proof of all that she had tasted of the tree of the knowledge of good and evil, and that she was under the influence of the same feeling as that which prompted Eve to hide herself when she discovered that she was fair. Mrs. Marl was not the most sympathetic of listeners, but Robina had never felt prompted to conceal anything from her mother before. But now it seemed *impossible* to make open and plenary confession. Perhaps she had an intuitive sense that she had taken a sudden leap into a world whither her mother could not follow her. Mrs. Marl had unbounded faith in her "system" as applied to her daughter's bringing up, but Nature has a way of setting at nought the most admirable systems, and if it should turn out that the fledgeling which the hen has kept within the coop should have been hatched from a duck egg, and should adventure itself on the surface of the deceitful lake as soon as it sees the water, what is the hen to do? Robina's mother would not have admitted the existence of instincts in one of her brood which come under the heading of "unregulated," and Robina dare not tell her towards what treacherous depths she felt herself drawn. Besides, there was something in her mother's nature that was antagonistic to the merest semblance of an adventure. Spontaneity, or what the French call the *imprévu*, was her aversion. She believed, as we have seen, in employment—unceasing and regular—not that she objected to "healthy exercise," provided it were taken in due time and season. But there should have been hours for drill and dancing, as there were hours for sleeping and eating. Moods were not to be consulted, excepting in the study of grammar. She would have made an almanac of each day's occupations for every man, woman, and child in the world, and contrived a routine of flower-wreathing and cocoa-nut-picking for the South Sea Islanders themselves. She was not entirely an illiberal woman, but disliked any departure from the established order of things. *Work, work*, was her *mot d'ordre*; her favourite quotation was that

> *Satan finds some mischief still*
> *For idle hands to do.*

In the insect world she would have taken her place among those ants that are always seen hurrying along with a burden which they never seem to deposit anywhere. A little younger, a little less angular in form, she might have served for the model of La Fourmi.[9] Her activity gave all who lived with her a sense of unrest. Robina had been taught to think that to sit with her hands before her, doing nothing, was to commit a deliberate sin.

Acting upon this principle now, Mrs. Marl continued to drive her machine along with great energy, lamenting the fate of the cherry hat the while. It was true that she was obliged five minutes afterwards to undo all the stitches she had accomplished, but the end of "setting a good example" had been achieved. One motherly glance at the daughter to assure herself that she had escaped without hurt or scratch from the fangs of the retriever, one sigh of reassurance at the thought that she was whole in wind and limb, and the authoritative voice made itself heard once more.

"Bring down your last year's hat, child. You may unpick the flowers from it at once. I shall lodge a complaint at the police-station about that dog as soon as I have time. Come, make haste—there has been too much time wasted already."

But Robina did not make haste nor look for the "last year's hat" when she found herself at the top of the steep stairs, in the solitary attic that was her own domain. She walked straight to a small mirror suspended against the whitewashed wall. It was an uncompromising mirror, and it had been put into its place in a side-light—and an infinitely unflattering one—by the hands of Robina's mother. But, however uncompromising in intention, it could not throw back a harsh reflection of the face that looked into it now. What mirror could, in fact, when it is appealed to by anything so pretty as Robina? The most it could do was to confirm the triumph that the blue eyes and flushed cheeks had brought to it, and to repeat the tale that the squatter's eyes had been the first of all to tell. And she had longed only half an hour ago to be a cow!—with such a human body as this all the time in her possession! Robina, we may be sure, did not stop to think of all that the possession might entail.

She only smiled back at the image that she saw within the frame. A dispassionate observer would have seen in this very action the first fruits of the discovery she had made. A physiognomist might have gone further, and considered the softness of her features and the impressionable temperament they betrayed. Her lips were full and red, her chin white and rounded; but they lacked the lines that we associate with force of will; her nose was a charming little nose that could not be said to "turn upwards" in the brutal acceptation of the term, but only looked capable of doing something of the kind under great and unwarrantable provocation. But all these were but secondary attractions. It was in her eyes, like stars, set perhaps a little too close together, but blue as mountain lakes, and darkened by the natural blackness of the black fringe that surrounded them, that her chief beauty lay. As for expression, she was still at the age when the world, as we find it, is reflected in our faces. Until ten minutes ago it had lacked at least the element of self-consciousness.

The sovereign and the card were in the pocket into which she had slipped them when she went into her mother's presence. She put them now into the corner of a drawer wherein her birds' eggs, shells, woolwork, and the destructible property known as "keepsakes" were lying in unclassified heterogeneousness. She liked a look at the yellow gold, and the surface of the glazed card was so cool and smooth that she laid it against her warm cheek. But the result was not entirely satisfactory, and when she had thrown it into the drawer and closed it away from her with violence, she carried such troubled eyes into the darkening parlour, together with her last year's hat, that her mother's mind misgave her. "Are you *quite* sure you are not hurt, my child?" she queried anxiously, but Robina only shook her curly head. She was telling herself that after she had put the sovereign into the plate, and perhaps, after the Confirmation was over, she would, without fail, tell her mother all about everything.

HOW A CLAIM WAS NEARLY JUMPED
IN GUM-TREE GULLY

For the first time for ten years—a long period in the history of a country that can look back upon its lawless past of less than thirty years ago—sounds associated with human life were to be heard in Gum-tree Gully. Where only the magpie had hitherto tuned his voice in his own grotesquely melodious key, and pretentious native companions had not been afraid to stand in a ludicrous row, where kangaroos had hopped and nibbled, nervously alert without cause, while their little ones took headers in and out of their pouches unconcernedly, and lithe snakes had projected their quivering bodies fearlessly through the scrub—hard-handed men and women began to make their way. Gum-tree Gully, worthless from an auriferous point of view, had capabilities of its own for cultivation, and Gum-tree Gully was open for selection.

How it acquired its name, in a district where every gully is made up, more or less, of gum-trees, is a matter to be chronicled. There are "gums and gums," and the early explorers of Gum-tree Gully had testified to their appreciation of differences in trees, as we mark our appreciation of differences in people.

The veteran gum-tree, which had sufficed, on its own merits, to give its name to a range of country some miles in extent, grew close to the bed of one of the many creeks that may be credited with an equivocal share in the progenitorship of the River Coliban. Its claims to military honours were at least as well founded as those of any royal heir-apparent who has never seen a battle, or any fancifully martial princess who coquets with her sword and rides about in her dainty uniform on review days. I do not go so far as to say that if its claims had been brought before a colonial

Duke of Cambridge they would have been precisely examined into, or that a medal would thenceforth have depended from one of its splattered branches. But supposing a committee of arboriculturists, in these days of stamping out all the joyous old pantheistic customs, were to sit in open-air conclave and adjudge the reward of a caressing parasite to the sturdiest old trunk in the Australian bush, this ancient gum-tree would have been entwined for its remaining decades—years are of little account in the life of such a tree—by the very Abishag of a creeper.[10]

What of unseen warfare it had sustained could only be found out by noting in its uppermost branches, where a stump or a splintered jag betokened the loss of a limb. But these were small tributes to pay to the force of contending winds that had broken the backs of all the frailer trees around. It was easy to see what of resistance it had made by looking up its majestic trunk. There was a grand assurance in the rigidity of its uprightness, a calm self-assertion in its uncompromising straightness, as if, poised upon circumvagant roots, that, in exploring the quartzy soil, had curled themselves around a layer of primeval granite, it knew that nothing short of an earthquake which should have power to upheave the foundations of the hill itself could compel its stately body to the performance of any undue genuflexions.

Every succeeding season had stamped it with hieroglyphics of its own, to the interpretation of which only nature could furnish the key. Becoming warty as it reached maturity, and discharging its acrid juices less frequently than in its more expansive and full-blooded days, it had acquired a seasoned appearance as compared with the juvenile gums around it, that gave it all the dignity of a Chiron in the world of the Eucalypti.[11] A close examination of its seared back would have brought to light a succession of short horizontal indentations, succeeding each other at somewhat irregular intervals from about four feet above the ground to within a few feet of its first throwing out of a branch—a proof that, if time is to be measured by impressions, the gum-tree was older than the most aged oak in Britain—for what English tree can remember a time when naked savages scaled it, and scooped out hollows for the reception of their monkey-toes? Fresh bark had grown around these scars, very much as the skin grows over our childish cuts and wounds, at which we look in more advanced life, on being told that our bodies have been all transformed the while, wondering what we have in common with the absurd little being who lay awake half the night in anticipation of a new pocket-knife, and mutilated himself with it in the morning. Only that the impression has left its mark on the mind as distinctly as the knife has left its mark on the body, such a being, we would say, had passed away altogether.

Besides the indentations afore-mentioned—not to be twisted by the most acute decipherer of cuneiform inscriptions into signifying anything more than *points d'appui* for aboriginal fingers and toes—there were some characters inscribed on the opposite side of the tree, which favoured the supposition that they were channels for the outlet of an idea. A close inspection would have left, moreover, no doubt as to the original intentions of the artist. There was evidence of a lop-sided cross, laboriously cut into the very substance of the trunk. In lieu of the arms of a crucified Saviour, a capital D of lean proportions stood at the left-hand transverse extremity of the cross. Similarly, at the right-hand extremity, a letter of unsteady build, which could only be allowed to pass for a T on the hypothesis that it could have been intended for nothing else, balanced the capital D.

Above this ornamental design the successful designer had proudly cut out the popular representation of a heart—apparently in an advanced state of fatty degeneration. There was further proof of a desire on his part to portray the heart transfixed by a sharp instrument; but the difficulty of the perspective having overcome him at this point, he had launched out into *basso-relievo*, as was testified by the

43

fraction of a splint, inserted into a small hole that had been drilled in the very centre of the inflamed heart.

Upon these mysterious signs many outward forces had been brought into play. The rain had guttered down them; black ants had established an emigration depôt in their midst; opossums had scratched at them in running up the tree. It could not be supposed to matter to any one in the world that they should be obliterated altogether. In fact, if it had not been for the juxtaposition of the cross and the heart, the letters D.T. might mean nothing more than a waggish commemoration of a carouse, held in the early digging days under the shadow of the majestic gum.

Very few people passed by them. For the chance "sun-downer" who cast his tired eyes upon them, they could not signify much. Trees tell no tales of the emotions they have been witness to, otherwise every novelist who walks about the woods might fill his volumes without trouble. The letters had, then, apparently no mission to fulfil, other than the unsought-for one of serving for rainducts and ant colonies. As they became gradually more indistinct, even the swagmen, who, for the most part, were not great readers, took no heed that they were there. It might be, nevertheless, that an accident would bring them into prominence. They were as weather-beaten as the tree itself when the first selectors began to file through Gum-tree Gully, with their train of sheep and bullocks and canvas-covered carts. This was quite another race from the diggers. Plodders, in a great measure, who saw no lottery-box in the uncultivated bush; but a home in prospective, to be fought for, inch by inch, with the stony soil. For the most part these pioneers were young. The courage to begin at the beginning is lacking in middle age; never-theless, they comprehended the inevitable sprinkling of unsuccessful colonists—the men who are always too late at a "rush", who always appear on the scene of action just when the good time is over, who are struggling at home when they ought to be in Victoria, and struggling in Victoria when they ought to be in Queensland.

Gum-tree Gully was only faintly lighted by the waning after-effects of a brilliant sunset, when one of those disappointed ones, himself on the wane, pulled up his cart under the legendary gum-tree, and looked solemnly aloft into its far-seeing leaves. There is no prolonged crepuscular glow after sun-down in Australia. The sun disappears in a gorgeous nest of varying colours, and long after the vivid carmines have died out the sky retains a faint impression of them, and borders the tops of the hills with semi-tints of green and rose, like the inside of a shell. But down in hollows it is dark. The light ceases abruptly, and the opal line in the far-off horizon is the last lingering protest of daylight against the stars that are beginning to hurry to the front and pierce the cool atmosphere with more or less of silver or gold, according to their separate individualities.

Gum-tree Gully had probably seen its unruly days in the period when Melbourne was described by contemporaneous writers of the "Society for the Propagation of Christian Knowledge" school as "a wicked city; there is no city in the world so wicked as Melbourne." But, purified by the solitary contemplation of the "pearly gates of heaven," it evoked no associations unbefitting virgin soil in the minds of the well-intentioned workers on the way to their selections, whose highest aim in life was probably to establish themselves on their 320 acres as "boss cockatoos".

Such associations as it evoked for the middle-aged selector, standing in front of his cart, with the last red rays suffusing his face, were all centred in the gum-tree. His face was so irradiated, as he turned it round after his lengthy survey, that his mate, not prone to personal observation, felt it incumbent upon him to inquire, in an aggrieved sort of way, into the cause.

"Seems like as if you'd struck a patch, Dave!" he said, putting his pipe into his pocket, and working his way out through timber and hen-coops to the front, by way of seeing where the luck lay.

So he had, but it was not a divisible patch.

He had struck his bygone youth and heart's desire. In the malformed capitals, the cross dropping crystallised gum, the fading heart, he had struck the spectre of all his hopes and aims. It confronted him now and he bared his grizzled head before it. In a way, the letters and he had kept pace together. They were not more misshappen than his path in life. They were typical of all his undertakings. But they had endured, and he had endured. There *had* been a time, then, when he had felt as if success were possible to him.

In reply to his mate's comment, he pointed to the tree with the butt-end of his whip, putting on his wide-awake the while with dreamy air. His mate was in the habit of making allowances for him. Dave, according to his estimate, had "no more savvy than a child, but you never got a rough word out of him," and his learning was patent to all who found their friend's calligraphy a stumbling-block to the due enjoyment of their letters. But this was conduct that required checking. A man was not to be called from his sleepy corner and his pipe and fooled into staring at a rotten tree with its head in the clouds like Dave himself!

It was with sarcastic politeness that Dave's mate indicated the tree by a fine flourish of the right hand as he gravely inquired, "You're prospecting, I s'pose, Mister?"

Dave's face was still illuminated by the sunset as he rejoined, "That's just what it is; I'm prospecting."

"First time I ever heard tell of prospecting up a gum-tree. I'd like to know now what 'ud be the vally of gold. Say, Dave, I think I'll jump your claim."

"'Tisn't a claim as any one can jump," answered Dave. He looked fondly at the defaced inscription, and muttered softly, "Dave and Tilly"—there was something about the sound of the words that must have satisfied his fullest sense of euphony. After they had camped down for the night— Dave rolled up in his grey blanket at the very foot of the tree like a mammoth caterpillar—he reiterated at long intervals, in whispered inflections, "Dave and Tilly," "Dave and Tilly". "Dave and Tilly" were apparently the talismanic words that made of Dave a lion of labour. Gum-tree Gully soil demanded work of a sort to make a Hercules ponder. If only a new Amphion could have piped to the gums and brought them trooping down to the side of the creek, the rest of the work would have been easy.[12] It was the grubbing up of the monstrous stumps that clung by their hundred roots to the soil beneath the river-bed itself that took it out of Dave and his mate. They worked silently, devastating, as is prescribed by nature, that they might regenerate. Dave was a destroying angel among the trees. There are still to be seen in Gum-tree Gully stark grey gums, dead and leafless, that look with their rung trunks like the bowstrung corpses of malefactors. When the moon shines on these ghosts of trees, it is as if the end of life had come, and a dreary dead world were illumined by the non-vivifying light left in another dead world.

There was a triumph in felling the tallest gums. Dave's mate was fain to admit within himself that it was not he who struck the hardest blows. He tried to account for this contradiction according to his lights. "Was it a put-up game on Dave's part before?" He had always thought him a bit soft, but this looked like artfulness. He worked the harder for his perplexity, hammering his doubts into whatever he took in hand. Gum-tree Gully can testify to the prodigies that may be accomplished by a couple of sound men, who, by a rare chance, do not drink, and who work—each to his utmost—the one from motives only known to himself, the other from pride. There were queer hypotheses afloat. It was reputed that they were deadly enemies, and that each had made a vow to kill the other from overwork. But they worked on.

There was only one point at issue between them. Dave's mate, chopping on one occasion at the monumental gum-tree, found his wrist seized from behind by fingers hard as flexible steel. He dropped his axe, as if he had been committing an act of desecration, and turned round apologetically. Dave's pensive eyes were aflame. His careworn face was rejuvenated by the fervour of his sudden wrath.

"Don't you go for to do it, mate," he said, half threateningly; "don't you go for to do it. You know better than that!"

Dave's mate had at least ten years the advantage of him, but at that moment his conviction that he was the "better man of the two" received a shock. He remained sulkily dignified the whole of that day, only observing in a general sort of way, over the evening meal, as if he had been telling it in confidence to the quart pot in front of him, "that he would take to planting spuds; he'd had about enough of working like a nigger. If he couldn't hack at all the blasted timber on the creek he'd let it rip; he was full up of your *close* people; you never knew where to have them; he was open as the day himself," &c.

Dave waited patiently for the end of this somewhat pointed soliloquy, and put out his hand humbly.

"Don't you take it ill of me," he asked; "that writin's been as good as a prophecy to me. It's going on for twelve years since I wrote it, and it's been struggle and disappointment ever since. That cross, you see, 's got betwixt me and her, and it's kept us apart ever since. But when I come upon the old letters, unawares, the other day, I took fresh heart. It seemed like as if they were waitin' to come true. I've always kept the one wish in my mind, and I don't know now but what it may come off. Any way, so long as I've got the tree to look at I keep thinking so!"

Such a long speech for taciturn Dave took due effect. That his mate was mollified was evident from his looking higher than the quart pot, and addressing himself with a show of condescension to Dave himself. Only, having a nature not quite so transcendental for his own part, he sought to give the conversation a practical turn, and call things by their right names.

"T.'ll be a young woman, I expect?"

"That's it," replied Dave, deprecatingly.

"And you was goin' to be fixed off so soon as you'd get a streak o' luck?"

"Well, we were pledged to one another before I come out from the old country."

Dave's mate pulled out his triangular slice of tobacco and settled himself against the back of the tent, as one who was about to continue his catechism at his ease.

"Is T. settin' still a-waitin' for you?"

"She gave me her sacred word she'd wait till I'd get a home for her."

"And she's been waitin' all this time?"

"All this time!"

"Why didn't you bring her along with you at the start?"

"Well, she hadn't been brought up to rough it, as you may say," Dave explained, "and latterly I'd been losin' heart. I told her when I wrote to her—nigh upon two years back it is now—if it was to break my heart I couldn't justify it to myself to see her wait no longer. And after that I wouldn't so much as send her my address, so I couldn't get no more letters from her."

The tobacco was cut, and Dave's mate was pressing it into his evening pipe—so absorbed apparently in the work of ramming in more than the pipe could conveniently hold, that Dave plunged afresh into his explanation.

"It's come to my knowledge since I come here that she's just as I left her. I think if I could get a bit of a homestead fixed up down by the creek, that writin' mightn't be for nought after all—there's no telling!"

The pause that followed, only broken by the shrill chorus of the clamorous locusts, was awful. The romance of Dave's youth and middle age, avowed with a pathetic timidity which seemed to deprecate the treasuring of a romance at all, would have seemed less incongruous if some encouragement had been given, some reply audible, other than the intermittent puffs at the pipe.

But this was a case in which it behoved Dave's mate to be oracular. He waited until Dave's humiliation was complete before he spoke.

"You can't do more nor chance it. If it's for better, why,

it'll be for better; and if it's for worse, well, it'll be for worse, and that's putten' it straight."

The oracle had spoken. Oracles are like the counsels of time-servers. You may accept them very much as you please. They allow of as free an interpretation as most inspired sayings, being ambiguous enough to satisfy all elucidators of the meanings of prophecy.

Whatever gratitude Dave might have felt for this comprehensive exposition of his case he expressed by a gesture of acquiescence. Shrinking more than ever into himself, as was his wont, after any unlooked-for burst of extemporaneous confidence, he baffled his mate's well-meant endeavours to lead up to the subject of the tree. Gum-tree Gully was only aware that all along the bed of the creek the twisted trunks of the native trees were lying prone, and that, solitary, a giant gum stood, massive, tapering, grey, like a petrifaction for seventy feet from the ground, and thereupon breaking into a rustling mass of shining dark foliage—a leafy fountain through which the sunbeams pricked dancing holes of light into the shadow below. Further, that the eccentric selectors, who felled in earnest as Gladstone is credited with felling in sport, had built round the foot of the giant gum a sort of brush fence, within which the elder man of the two had been seen one moonlight night, his face, to all appearance, resting against the rugged bark. Verdict—"They were a queer lot."

During the succeeding season the influence of the writing was as marked as if it had been traced by a spirit hand. It was especially perceptible in the building of the house. If "Tilly" was all Dave's, Dave's mate might claim a joint-proprietorship in the "T." If Dave pondered with tender forethought before fixing the position of the front door, weighing the rival influences of a sunrise that seemed the harbinger of a rose-coloured day, and a sunset that turned the creek into a new Pactolus with golden edges,[13] Dave's mate had an intuitive perception of the way in which T. would "shape" with regard to the stacking of the chimneys.

It was he who shingled the roof, from a preconceived certainty that T. was not the kind to be put off with galvanised iron; it was he who carted the hardwood boards from the township for the flooring of the verandah, having settled it to his own satisfaction that it would not do to "foist any of your clay flooring upon T." There was a promise of permanence in every nail that was driven into every plank. It is the idea which governs—not the fact. The secret of the potentiality of the old gum-tree was not even known to the selector and his mate. If it had been explained to them that all this sinew-stretching and muscle-pulling work was a straining after the ideal, they would not have understood it. But it was nothing else. The best work that has ever been done has always been done in response to it; for it is the only work into which is put the truest part of oneself. If the veriest atheist feels devotional perforce when he looks up at a sublime spire piercing the hazy blue far over his head, or hears an excursive burst of high, sweet melody in the middle of a midnight mass, it is not, as he will explain to you, because his senses of sight or hearing are suddenly taken by storm, but because through these senses the intense spirit of the artificer or the musician impresses him with a reflection of its absorbing devotion. The part left in the spire or the music will make itself heard while the world lasts.

It was during the Christmas week of 187–, at a time when the Victorian landscape was enlivened by the canary-coloured patches of ripening crop, that Dave's mate drove the fresh-painted cart over to the township to meet Dave and his wife. The newly-engaged young lady at the Commercial Hotel, in whose unabashed eyes his manly face and figure, toned down in their tendency to fleshiness by his fat-repressing work, had found favour, smirked behind the bar as she saw him rein up in the yard. In the bright green of the cart and the bright scarlet of his tie, set off by the cheerful uniformity of his new slop suit, she saw delicate evidences of his intentions. We are so apt to think that every falling shower has its designs against us, or for us, as the case may be, that it was natural enough on the part of the young person at the Commercial to see in these details a something bearing directly upon herself. She adopted forthwith her most insinuating expression, and threw it away, after all, on a half-tipsy swagman, blind of one eye; for Dave's mate, after a word with the groom, passed straight out of the yard, and stationed himself at the corner of the street, there to watch for the arrival of Cobb and Co.'s coach.

The mystic T. was about to assume the shape of a flesh-and-blood woman. Dave's mate fidgeted under the heated verandah in front of the general store; his temples were throbbing as if he had been working in the sun with his hat off. The prospect of finding the coach packed with a whole harem consigned to him alone could not have excited him more than the advent of the newly-married wife of another man. No special houri, before whose particular charms Dave's mate would certainly have been the first to abase himself, could quite have taken the place of the T. whose unseen presence had encouraged him for so long— in deference to whose divined inclinations he had shingled the house and floored the verandah. Not that he was at all likely to tell himself anything of the sort. There is no possible analysis of sentiment without education. He probably told himself that the coach was late, and that he'd been "gaping down the road a devil of a time." The *ennui* of standing about was beginning to tell in favour of the young lady behind the bar of the Commercial, and Dave's mate had already turned his back to the verandah and the corner, when an intermittent rattle in the distance made him pause. His hardihood went away on the spot. Any one seeing the sheepish expression on the face of the big brown-bearded man in the slop suit would never have given him credit for fancying himself to the extent indulged in under ordinary circumstances by Dave's mate. The coach came tilting along from the bush track on to the macadamized road, with a jingling and a clattering of appalling force. A puff of north wind threw the dust right ahead into the wide-open eyes of Dave's mate, and by the time he could see out of them again the coach had drawn noisily up at the side of the pavement, and Dave, with the very look his mate remembered when they had first come upon the gum-tree, was holding out his hand from the inside. Next to him was the top of a woman's brown hat. The coach-door being opened, Dave descended first, and turning quickly round, held out his arms to the woman in the brown hat. He jumped her out like a child, and she stood, with her head reaching no higher than his shoulder, quite close to him on the pavement. And now Dave's mate saw his creation materialised. A small-faced, sallow woman, inexpressibly neat all over, with large eyes and white teeth, and a *pose* foreign to Gum-tree Gully belles, with dark plaits just showing on their smooth surface a chance grey hair, and a slight round waist, and a small round throat. Dave's mate had a sudden perception of the loudness of his tie which hampered the freedom of his greeting. It made him almost ashamed to think of the green cart. He had never "fancied himself" so little before.

"It's my mate," was all Dave said by way of introducing him. "I put you first, you see, Tilly, and he comes second."

Tilly held out an ungloved cool little hand that almost made him laugh. It felt like nothing but a tiny squirrel. He shook it with exceeding care, not knowing how strong a pressure of his horny muscular hand it was safe to bestow upon it. As to saying anything, that was quite out of the question. But Tilly had a woman's secret for putting him at ease. She looked up into his face from under her brown hat, and made her large shining eyes say to him in so many words, "You please me, don't you see? and I want to please you in my turn."

She had looked so at Dave years ago—he believed for his own part that she had never looked so at anybody else—and she had found occasion to practise the look during his absence a few scores of times at least, which accounted for its coming so readily. But to Dave's mate it was a new sort of experience. The "minauderies"[14] of the young lady at the Commercial were quite another thing from this soul and sense quelling glance. He was not even aware as yet whether he was beholden to her for it or no. The T. he had toiled for could never come back again; but already he was not sure that he would change it for the living "Mrs. Dave".

Tilly was a born woman of the world. On being hoisted up into the green cart she sat on a high plank between her husband and his mate, her toes barely touching the bottom, as much at her ease as if she were a little sister whom they were bringing home for the holidays. She asked questions in a demure way, knowing that they would both answer at once; and feigned to be delightfully "new-chummish," by way of making them laugh. For all that, they had never been alive to the beauties of the bush track before, having hurried up, as a rule, to get back to work. But when Tilly sniffed at the aromatic odour of the gums and peppermints, blown into their faces by the cool evening breeze, standing right up to watch a flight of "blue mountains" swooping through the air, and pushed back her brown hat to remark upon the funny colour of the range of hills ahead of them—which, indeed, were turning from slate-colour to delicate mauve in the sunset—they took note of these facts for the first time, all the while naïvely convinced that they were "showing Tilly the ropes."

This was the way with them at first. It should have been the way with them always. But then Dave's mate should have been a Sir Galahad, and Tilly a woman without eyes, and Dave himself anything but the simple-hearted being he was.

Gum-tree Gully was witness at first to a trinity in unity. Where an incorporeal presence had given a spur to physical effort, a light-footed woman moved about all day. In spite of Dave's fears on the score of her power of "roughing it",

Tilly might have been born to look after a bushman's home; to bake in a camp oven, to carry her weekly wash to the river-side, and twitter along with the birds over her wash-tub. But if a woman, in the prime of her life, is to be helpmate to two men, she should be at least a Metis (wisest of all the daughters of gods and men), or they should be blind, or one of them should be willing to go by the "steep and thorny way to heaven." Failing these alternatives the trinity at Gum-tree Gully must inevitably have its term.

It came to no tragical end. Mrs. Dave was mending the socks of the selectors indiscriminately under the shadow of the gum-tree. She had arranged each heap with regard to its separate owners, nattily, as was her fashion of doing things, when, a darker shadow enveloping her, she looked up with a start. Dave's mate, his face white as if he had been drinking, came hastily up to her and laid violent hands on his particular pile of socks. He picked them up without so much as looking at her, and as he almost turned his back upon her in speaking, she had some ado to make out the purport of his few hurried words.

"It's about time for me to clear out," she heard; "if I wasn't a fool I'd have cleared out at the first—and that's all about it!"

"Oh my!" said Tilly, "you're not going to leave us?"

There was a dismayed note ringing in her accent. Dave's mate turned round, and encountered her upturned eyes, pleading from beneath the rim of the travelled brown hat—those eyes that had done all the mischief from the beginning! He looked as severe as if his heart had not been sinking to sickness. "Yes, I am," he said huskily, "and I guess you know why!"

Her eyes wandered inquiringly over his face.

"Have you had words with Dave?"

"Not I. I don't s'pose you think I have neither."

"Oh, then, *why* do you go?"

There was no actual guilt to be laid at the door of Dave's wife, but perhaps it was just as well that Dave was not at hand to see the expression in her steadfast eyes as she slowly repeated the words, "Why—do—you—go?"

Dave's mate found that his knees were trembling. They would have given way in another instant, and he would have fallen down upon them in front of Mrs. Dave, but looking up in the desperation of his mental tussle, the rude letters on the gum-tree confronted him as plainly as if they had been traced in fire by the finger which threw confusion into the hearts of the Babylonian revellers in olden times. From this moment he looked down no more. There was not a turn in the D or the T which was not somehow characteristic of Dave. His blunders, his simplicity, and his goodness seemed to cry out against treachery from the twisted cross and the half-obliterated heart.

He had said, in reply to his mate's joke on his new sort of gold discovery, "'Tisn't a claim as any one can jump!" never taking into account that his claim was a human one, and humanity false. But Dave's mate remembered it all.

"I'd be stopping on for no good," he replied, always looking straight ahead of him at the tree. "There's no two words about it. Maybe I'll see you again—by'nd-by—anyhow, I wish you luck."

He was gone before she could put out her hand, or even call up another of her wonderful glances. She sat, thinking, under the tree long after he had left her. It was all but dark when her husband came out to call her in, and found her still, pensive, in the same place. No one could have been tenderer of her; but of Dave's tenderness she had not been hitherto as ambitious as was compatible with wifely sentiment. She smiled at him now, lowering her eyes, and listening with head turned partly aside, but without comment, to his disjointed observations touching the departure of his mate.

"He hasn't been the chap he used to be, latterly. It seems to me like as if there was something on his mind—and that 'ud work on him, d'ye see—for I've never known him to keep a thing to himself all the years we've lived together.

I said as much, mind you, as I'd give the best part of the farm to have him stop; and he up and says, 'Do you want to cut your own throat?' quite savage-like. There was no holding him after that, but I doubt he's got something on his mind, as I said before. . . . But there's only one good can come of it, as fur as I can see—I've got my little woman all to myself.''

It must have been nothing more than a chance streak of moonlight which filtered at that instant through the black gum-leaves, silvering the bark and the old inscription, and softening Tilly's face to penitence. Still, it could not have been a moonbeam that she wiped away with a furtive gesture of her small palm, before giving her hand to Dave and passing out with him from under the shadow of the tree into the light of the home within.

BARREN LOVE

I

Only two veins standing out from a woman's neck—that was all! The cynic told himself he was a fool, and telling himself so, walked away to the farther end of the deck. Blue veins starting up from a young throat! There was nothing, after all, in a phenomenon of the sort—nothing, that is to say, that could not be explained on physiological grounds. The cynic was accustomed to look at manifestations of pain from a point of view purely scientific. Thus, when you cut off the head of a dog-fish, the monster squirms with the agony. Like the evil it typifies, there is a hold-fastness in its grip of life. But you know, or you believe you know, of how much account is all this resistant wrestling with death! What softer sensation do you have than one of animosity towards the dog-fish for dying so hard, and for giving you such a world of trouble to get your blunt knife through a neck like animated indiarubber?

The cynic admitted a difference between the throat of a placoidian and the throat of a young girl. But to watch the one gasping its death-gurgle from a bleeding gash, and the other, distorted, working against a sentimental grief, might not of itself be a process provocative of intensely differing emotions. The cynic, holding it as a theory that softening of the heart and softening of the brain have meanings almost synonymous, pooh-poohed his maudlin fancies, and walked resolutely back to his old post by the bulwarks. Those obtrusive veins annoyed him! In thirty or forty years' time they might ride up, if they chose. Everything should be smooth in youth, even to the trunk of a tree. Nature had given these veins a semi-opaque covering, smoother and softer than the blossom of an arum. In their normal condition they obliterated themselves behind it, or only started into the

59

faintest show of self-assertion when their home was unsettled. And here they had risen like blue weals, raised by the lash of an inward thong!

The cynic, feeling justified in his irritation, looked up from the demonstrative neck to the face above it—and immediately walked away. This time it was for good. He felt about as much ashamed of himself as if he had torn open the girl's dress and asked her where she was smarting.

Not that the cynic was unacquainted with the nature of tears—"a limpid fluid secreted by the lachrymal gland," &c. If you come to tears, nothing can shed them more profusely than a seal. The soft-eyed creature wails and cries on the score of her outraged maternity. She plants her unwieldy body in front of her little one and asks for mercy with streaming eyes. Tears, therefore, are nothing in themselves! Sterne shed them by the bucketsful, with much maudlin satisfaction to himself the while. The cynic loathed Sterne, and despised the sentimentalist for his perpetual flourish of handkerchiefs in the faces of his readers.[15] But on the present occasion he came very near to despising himself. He wondered just when he would forget the strained eyes—every gleam of self-consciousness washed out of them—nothing but an intelligence of suffering left. He did not require to be told that from among the departing boats, fast turning into mere buoyant dots in the distance, one more than another must have magnetised the hopeless gaze.

Looking half-way across Plymouth harbour, by the light of a sudden burst of yellow sunshine, he could discern the outline of a man standing upright in the foremost boat of all.

The cynic was so quick in connecting the dejection of the man's attitude with the crushed aspect of the girl, that he would have despised himself with a fresh access of vigour if it had occurred to him to think about himself in the matter at all. Somehow, he forgot at the moment to make proper sport of his own show of human interest. The fluttering of a handkerchief in the boat called forth a curious corresponding signal on the part of the girl. Her hands, trembling all over, like the rest of her body, tugged at her collar-fastening and extracted a hidden white envelope. They carried it to her lips— she was past all heed of curious bystanders long ago! The passionate kissing of the unheeding paper—the stretching of it out towards the boat, as if so frantic a gesture might stay even the stolid Plymouth boatman—the effort that she made to restore it to its place and lay it as a sort of healing plaster against her gasping throat—all this might have been grotesque if it had been only one shade less humanly real. The cynic found a characteristic outlet for his unaccountable sensations by glaring with an expression of appalling severity at any unwary waif who might venture within three yards of the desolate girl. Long after the boat was out of sight she continued to stand in the same spot, stonily indifferent to the scene before her. For the last English sunset was sending the ship on her way in a rose-coloured light. People on the Plymouth pier saw her in a haze of burnished mist, moving airily away under gilded sails.

II

The cynic, who was not called Mr. Cynic, however, by those on board, but Mr. Ralph Grimwood, or Mr. Grimwood only, was very sea-sick. Between the intervals of his degradation he thought about dog-fishes and seals; he thought about the affections too—those perplexing equivalents in the sum total of the disturbing influences that control us. On principle, he execrated the affections—officious meddlers in the sound mechanical functions of the body. On principle, he was antagonistic to love, the mere display of which would have been nauseous if it had not been so ludicrous! But sea-sickness, it would seem, had rendered him illogical. As he lay in his bunk, careful not to look at the swinging port-hole, a mere glance at which seemed to heave him up into the watery clouds and drag him down into the watery depths, he fell to picturing what his life might have become if he could have changed personalities with the vague outline in the boat. Being weakened by so much diminution of bile, he was fain to indulge the fancy. He had never known what it was to be light-headed as yet. Instead, therefore, of controlling his impulse, according to his stern creed, he was constrained to let his impulse control him. And it controlled him utterly!

Now he could see the boat racing after the ship, while he himself was urging it on! Now he could see himself climbing up the ship's side, clothed always in the shadowy form he had distinguished. How soon he had kissed back into their white hiding-place the poor swollen veins! He had separated the helpless hands twisted into each other for their own support, and put them round his strong, surly shoulders. His lips had closed for one instant the heavily-weighted eyelids, that he might see the grey eyes open again with such a look as his touch would have restored to them. It need not be pointed out that the light-headed fancy was running riot through his brain.

Meanwhile a wind had set in that was driving away all traces of tears from the emigrant's cheeks, and blowing a fresher brininess against them instead. The ship, at the outset, swayed timorously along, like a child in leading-strings. The wind pushed her about, slapped her alternately on either side, tilted her forward, and hitched her back, till she jerked like a jibbing horse—finally took her by the hand and pulled her smoothly along across the Bay of Biscay. Then Mr. Grimwood came on deck.

The passengers up above were proudly displaying their newly-acquired sea-legs. They strutted along uncertainly, after the manner of ducks,—very much pressed for time to get nowhere at all. Mr. Grimwood watched them stumping past him, the same strained expression peculiar to landsfolk at the outset of a long voyage, stamping them all; the rims of their eyes reddened by the wind.

The deck was a flush one, and amid-ships was a balustrade dividing the spaces allotted respectively to the first and second-class passengers. As it is always easier to lower one's social status than to raise it, on board ship as in the world, passengers from the first cabin were allowed the run of the space paid for by passengers from the second cabin. None of them, however, with the sole exception of Mr. Grimwood, seemed in any especial hurry to snatch at their privilege. Probably it was one of the cynic's eccentricities to like whiffs of a mixed character.

On the second-class deck the nostrils conveyed food to the mind in the shape of a hundred conjectures. For instance, on the weather side, it was impossible, after a few enforced sniffs, to abstain from speculations as to the state in which the fowls might be kept. On the lee side, the speculative mind might find a still wider range and lose itself in dwelling on the odoriferous origin of ship's grease. It is not certain whether these inducements allured Mr. Grimwood from the quarter-deck. If neither fowls nor ship's grease attracted him, it may be inferred that the people were worth a glance, albeit not from Mr. Grimwood's point of view—a cynic always sees a crumbling skeleton behind the most life-warm flesh.

They were of all varieties—the needy family man whose olive branches would have borne pruning, the runaway defaulter who looked even at the horizon with suspicion—the willing-to-better-herself spinster, who knew to a nicety how many of the ship's officers were married, and could have told off each mate to his watch on deck with less hesitation than the Captain himself. In none of these classes would you have included the one solitary passenger standing by herself on a coil of rope, with arms leaning on the bulwarks and eyes directed to the impalpable boundary-line of the sea. Neither would you have found her counterpart more readily among the first-class passengers. In the quiescence of her present attitude, as in the mute storminess of her grief, she seemed absolutely to ignore all human surroundings. Andromeda,[16] chained to a rock, with foam leaping over her white limbs, could not have been more oblivious of the impression she was conveying than was this plaid-enveloped girl.

Mr. Grimwood had cultivated art even before he cultivated cynicism. To a stirring of the ancient art-impulse within him he sacrificed his reflections anent dog-fishes and seals. With such a model for an Andromeda, his cynicism might all have spent itself on the Dragon. Who can say? It is certain that some of his bile had spent itself already. Andromeda would not, perhaps, have worn a black felt hat or a green plaid shawl; but could even Andromeda's hair have been blown back into softer, silkier rings from whiter temples; could Andromeda's eyes—always granting that they were of the same transparent grey—have been hedged in by longer lashes; could Andromeda herself have shown a purer profile, or—now that the mutinous veins were laid to rest—have displayed a more rounded throat? Mr. Grimwood, gravely parading the second-deck, must have known all this by intuition. It was soon after his excursive walk along the hen-coops that he was seen in conversation with the Captain.

That same afternoon, the second-class steward, who was washing second-class plates in second-class slop, was half-deafened by a call from the Captain himself. The steward was to fetch him the young woman in plaid—Miss Leighton by name—and to look sharp about it.

The Captain was a sort of typical tar—one of a race not quite extinct; still to be met with on old colonial wool-ships, despite the new genus introduced by steam. He did not think about Andromeda when he saw Miss Leighton, but it partly occurred to him that it was a blank shame such an eternally fine girl should be spooking about the world by herself. It seemed that he had summoned her to give her a cheering piece of news. It appeared, according to the Captain's story, that a letter and a deposit had been put into his hands at starting which, by some remarkable over-sight, had never been opened until to-day. The letter bore no signature—over this part of his story the Captain blundered unaccountably. Somebody, about whose appearance the Captain was by no means clear, had entrusted the letter to his keeping. In fact, only as regarded the instructions, did the Captain express himself with anything like clearness, and on that head he was more than explicit. Miss Leighton was to travel as a saloon passenger, the deposit being sufficient not only to defray the cost of her passage-money, but to give her a cabin to herself. Here the Captain attempted an apology for his delay in imparting the news. Somehow, he blundered again, and stopped suddenly short.

Certainly Miss Leighton's mind must have been given to travelling on its own account. All the time the Captain was speaking, it seemed to be journeying back from some dreary distance, until it shone through her great abstracted eyes. Their lost, desolate look made way for the light that a warm sense of surrounding care brought into them. It was no longer Andromeda with the horror of the Dragon's presence in her white face, but Andromeda with uplifted eyes watching the glittering pathway of her deliverer through the air.

Poetical justice should have awarded Mr. Grimwood a

seat next to Miss Leighton at the dinner-table, but poetical justice was not embodied in the head-steward—a ginger-hued little man, upon whom devolved the arrangement of the passengers' places. A constant suspicion that some outrage upon his dignity might be meditated had caused the little steward's eyes to protrude. His exalted position was a bar to his making any confidential friends. He was on speaking terms only with the cook, and spent his life with one eye upon the lazarete and the other on the look-out for a slight.

The cynic's post at the dinner-table was exactly in front of his cabin. When his eyes travelled along a row of ungainly noses on the same side of the table as his own, they invariably stopped at a small Greek profile, standing out like a cameo from among the irregular heads that flanked it. There was something embarrassing in looking down a column of strongly-defined nose-tips. The cynic waited until the regulation plum-duff was put into its place; then he took a rapid glance to the rear. Out of all the assortment of heads, there was only one that could possibly correspond to the profile— a stately little head, very black and shining, perhaps a shade too upright, as if the knot of heavy hair on the nape had pulled it ever so slightly back.

And through all the swinging about in the Bay of Biscay, Mr. Grimwood continued to take his daily glance. It was not, perhaps, so fruitful of consequences as a nearer approach to the Andromeda might have proved itself. Sympathies have declared themselves on board ship between young men and women in proximity at meal-time, which otherwise must have been everlastingly ignored. What will not a constant adherence to black-currant tart in two young persons of different sexes engender? How steel yourself against a growing interest in the possessor of a plate that accompanies your own with such unswerving fidelity?

Only that the cynic was like nobody else on board ship or elsewhere, he would not have sat daily with an afflicted dowager and a failing octogenarian on either side of him. He would have found means to install himself in the place of one of the nondescript spinsters who enclosed Miss Leighton. But being unlike anybody else in any respect whatever, it was entirely consistent with his character to make a point of avoiding her. As to analysing his motives, that is another thing. It is not pretended that any man's intimate feelings are open to dissection.

There have been natures sufficiently high-flown to set a flesh-and-blood statue on an ideal pedestal, and to shrink from seeing the statue come down to its regular meals. There have been natures, high-flown too, to whom the quintessence of beauty lies in the bloom which covers it. Perhaps, in the cynic's eyes, the mystery surrounding the luxury of Miss Leighton's position was the bloom that covered its solid good. There are yet other natures, and these are not necessarily high-flown, who argue that only one passion can move a woman to so intense an agony of grief as that of which the cynic had been witness. Were such a passion immediately transferable, at what value must the new recipient place it in the sum of human emotions? Its sweetness might be just as transitory as its grief—all a piece of unconscious play-acting. Now the list of possible reasons is quite exhausted, it is hardly necessary to repeat that the cynic was unlike anybody else. As for the present of the cabin, there have been precedents in this direction. Amelia Sedley played on the piano Dobbin had restored to her, with something of the feeling that comforted Miss Leighton when she closed her eyes in the new cabin that the George Osborne of her dreams had chosen for her.[17]

III

If Mr. Mantalini had ever been in the doldrums, he might have added to his experience of "demmed moist unpleasant bodies." A ship constrained to loiter there breaks out into a cold sweat. Everything she carries becomes clammy. In this respect there is not much difference between the animate and the inanimate bodies that she holds—unless it be that the first are pervaded with a warm stickiness, and the last with a cold stickiness. The most sanguineous of people assume the consistency of dough before it is kneaded. As for the spare folk, they look as if the scant supply of blood in their veins had turned to London milk. Then simple practical suggestions on the great question of "demand and supply" occur to those unversed in the rudiments of political economy. The balance between the internal and the external moisture must be maintained; in maintaining it, panting passengers are reminded of "Fair-shon's Son"—

> *Who married Noah's daughter,*
> *And nearly spoilt ta Flood*
> *By drinking up ta water.*

"Which he would have done," adds his sceptical chronicler—

> *. . . Had the mixture been*
> *Only half Glenlivet.*

In emulation of the patriarch's convivial son-in-law, passengers only temper their drink with the tepid water served in regulation quantities to all on board. It is calculated that a little tepid water is very satisfying. Niggards, who depend upon it entirely, not using it as a tempering medium, but as a pure draught, are not taken into account on board a sailing-ship. They cannot even act upon Mr. Barlow's sage advice, and only "drink when they are dry." For they are always dry, and there is nothing to drink.

Under all ordinary and everyday circumstances the usual lot of the niggard at sea would have fallen to Miss Leighton's share. The Turkish bath atmosphere had wrapped her round, as it had enveloped her fellows. The cynic could see that his marble Andromeda was fast turning into an Andromeda of alabaster. Alabaster needs more tender handling than marble. The deposit placed in the Captain's hands seemed to have become self-fertilising like an oyster. How else could it be that a friendless young woman, who had come on board with nothing but a second-class ticket, a pair of strange grey eyes, and a Grecian profile, should find all her wants guessed at and gratified, before she had had time to acknowledge them as wants at all? The pompous little steward "put himself in four" (as the French say) on her behalf. The easiest of easy-chairs was always in waiting for her, in the shadiest patch on deck so soon as the top of her straw-hat could be seen in the saloon beneath the skylight. While simmering dowagers wiped their faces, palm-leaf fans lay ready to hand, to beat away the too bold air resting in heavy heat on her pure cheeks. She could no longer look in the direction of the damp decanter with its freight of rusty warm water. So sure as she did so, the steward's eyes goggled at her meaningly. A moment later, in spite of all her laughing, wondering protestations, she was assailed with a whole battery of bottles. For peace's sake she was constrained to make choice from among the cool effervescent drinks drawn up before her. She was like Beauty in the enchanted palace, whose sensations were responded to as soon as they were born—but where was the Beast?

The mystification gave rise to the sweetest of day-dreams. Whether the mysterious guardianship was exerted, like an electric wire of love, from the home she had left—whether it was held by some loyally-loving soul on board, she could not so much as conjecture. It was always there—like a soothing magnetic influence. Sometimes she fancied it must be very close to her—only there was nobody exactly like the Beast on board. The cynic, to be sure, in his aloofness from his kind, had something of the untamed beast about him; but then he never came to her to be stroked. He spoke rarely, and his rare speech was only exchanged with two persons—the Captain, who was "boss" on deck, and the steward, who was "boss" down below.

By the time the ship had passed through the Tropic Belt most of the resources in the way of amusement had been exhausted. The Trades, in rescuing the vessel from the doldrums, had been so much in earnest, that before long they would launch her into the "roaring Forties" south of the Line. They had not quite abandoned her yet, but took her up and dropped her capriciously, treating her very much after the manner of a sovereign to a court favourite.

The cynic did not as yet admit to himself that he was well content they should drop her thus. He would never have allowed that, of his own accord, he indulged in the ridiculous visions that forced themselves upon him as he stood night after night intently watching the heaped-up glories in the west. Mad visions of finding the ship converted into a love-laden *Flying Dutchman* everlastingly sailing over such a glowing sea as this, to such an impalpable shore as the landscape in the clouds. With only one passenger, whom he would have chosen! The rest were for the most part sensible, prosaic folk, who would have looked properly disconcerted had it been suggested to them that, instead of sailing direct to Melbourne, they should make tracks for airy cities built up of glittering hues.

IV

The cynic did not drivel in the morning. It was his wont to wake himself early and think over a subject he had in his mind to write about. The subject was to bear upon the futility of giving the reins to the indulgence of the weakness called sentiment. He had his arguments all ready before coming on board. The perplexing part of it was, that although he was as much convinced of their soundness as ever, he did not see his way to putting them as clearly as he would have wished. He woke himself up on purpose to think of them at such an early hour, one morning in particular, that his ideas respecting sentiment were rather confused. They were mixed up with a sort of apathetic wonder at the noise of the swishing of water overhead. He supposed, lazily, that the middies must be washing the deck earlier than usual.

He felt no curiosity, however, about the change of time, being in the condition of sleepy receptiveness which makes everything indifferent to us. Neither did he trouble himself so far as to open his half-closed eyelids, even when a sort of red glare pervaded the darkness before them. Half-raising them at last, he saw—always with the same dream-like stolidity of gaze—that the sunrise seemed to illuminate his cabin in bursts of crimson light, and that the calm sea, lying tranquilly before his port-hole, was stained a deep carmine. He would have shut his eyes again on this phenomenon, if his sight had been the only sense appealed to. But a vigorous call was suddenly made upon his hearing and smelling perceptions as well.

Through the tarred planks over his head came the discordant sound of a woman's agonised scream—through the chinks and crannies of his cabin came a sickening scent of burning. Away went the thread of his argument against sentiment; away went the fag-end of his meaningless dream! As he bounded on to the cabin floor, a hundred trembling wretches, waking to so cruel a mockery of the morning sun, shrieked and raved to the Captain and the Omnipotent to save them from the flames.

Mr. Grimwood's cynicism ensured his keeping a cool head. One glance at the deck was enough to convince him that in a very few hours the ship would be nothing more than a flaming tar-barrel. The fire, he could see, must have been working in an underhand way in the hold, from the mouth of which it was coming up now as from the bottomless pit. There was something so sublime in its greed of prey, as it rolled up in scorching volumes of transparent blood-colour, that he stood watching it for a few seconds, unheeding the yells of the passengers.

There was a show being made of keeping the triumphant flames at bay, whereat they crouched like a panther preparing for a final spring. But Mr. Grimwood could see through this pretence from the first. The real work of the moment lay in the getting out of the boats for escape. But two of the boats were already useless, and the others could never have held the souls, all counted, on board. The cynic's theories about sentiment were strangely revolutionised as he went below and passed the open cabin-doors. Of all the distorted faces that he saw, how many would ever shape themselves into a laugh again?

The one cabin-door that he stopped at was ajar. In his hurry he hardly made a show of knocking before he pushed it open. Already there was a thin smoke spreading itself over the saloon. Inside the cabins the air was unnaturally warm. The cynic knew that all this was real. He knew that he had no more proprietorship over the girl he had come to save than he had over the ship itself. Yet it would have been just as easy to tell the upstart flames overhead to lie down and lick at empty space as to tell his own foolish heart to stop beating with unreasonable, exultant joy while he edged his way into the little cabin. He had hungered for it so often in his dreams—for just what had come to pass now! Only, as a dying man, he might speak without attuning his voice to a pitch of artificial coldness—he might look without dreading lest the love-light in his eyes should betray him. He had forced his way through with the one thought only uppermost in his mind. The sinister glare from above—the crackling noise of the flames as they ran around the mainmast—the ugly chorus of screams overhead—screams of vitality that will not be tortured out of being, and protests against surrendering itself: all these were ministers to his absorbing passion. Now that he had passed into the cabin, pity and tenderness for its occupant swallowed up the egotistic triumph.

She was crouched on her berth like one waiting; partly smothered up in the worn plaid shawl, an old-fashioned covering of modern date, invested with all the grace of ancient drapery in the cynic's eyes—partly wrapped round by layers of brightly-dark hair, that lost itself somewhere in the blankets beneath her. Through all the terror in her drawn face, there was a something of expectation in the startled eyes—a vague trust that the guardianship she had taken refuge in would not forsake her in this pass. It could not be that the unknown power so quick to divine her wants, to forestall her fancies, to humour her passing whims, should leave her here, until her white skin shrivelled away with the heat and her voice was strangled by the smoke in the middle of its prayer for help. She had not so much as uttered one cry as yet. When Mr. Grimwood made his way in she broke into a sob of relief.

"I knew you would come," she said. "You are come to take care of me!"

Perhaps if the goggle-eyed little steward had come in she would have said the same thing. Any one appearing at this crisis must be the embodiment of the invisible love that had cherished her. Only it is doubtful whether, even at this supreme moment, the red light could have transformed the perky expression of the little steward as it had transformed Mr. Grimwood's. Women's rights' champions are without doubt altogether right. They have no end of solid grievances to redress. Let them bring about—if they can—social, intellectual, and muscular equality between the sexes. There is a certain sentimental instinct they can never do away with—

the blind, unreasoning sense of comfort a trembling, frightened woman feels when a strong, earnest man takes her under his protection in a moment of danger.

There was such a volume of father-like, lover-like tenderness in Mr. Grimwood's tone as he came closer to reassure her—if the fire had curled itself round her doorway as the faint wreaths of smoke were beginning to curl she could not but have taken hope. He did not even hurry her unduly, though he knew that every second lost was a chance of life gone. He kneeled down by her berth—she had held out her hands to him as he came in—and holding her hands he spoke.

"She should go in the first boat," he told her; "the sea was so calm that the journey would be an easy one—they were within a hundred miles of Cape Town—he knew she was a brave girl and would do as he told her—he guaranteed to save her, but she must dress without loss of time—never mind what she put on—he would bring her a cloak and wraps from his cabin—in a minute he would be back again for her—only she must not lose any time."

He was happier than he had ever been in his life as he scrambled together the coverings in his cabin that were to protect her from the chill sea-air. He dived into his trunk for a small treasure-box filled with his money and valuables, and carried it out with the wraps. When he returned to Miss Leighton's cabin the saloon was already dusky with smoke. She was waiting for him, dressed as when she came on board, and held close to his arm as he piloted her through the tumult below to the deck.

She could not help clinging to him afresh, with a gasp of horror, when she saw the scene above. It is all very well for people to die when they are let down to it by long illness or age! To be forced out of life so summarily—to be whipped into the green deep water, from which all your body shrinks, by the tingle of an unnatural smart against your flesh, is enough to make you shriek and protest. To see your own belongings in the same plight is enough to make you blaspheme. As for the sense that your kind is suffering along with you—there is not much comfort to be got out of it. Companionship in the search for glory is quite another thing. Warfare is as much a preparation for death as an illness without the bodily attenuation. A company of soldiers incite each other to mount a breach. On board a burning ship there is no glory to be gained—no predominant feeling for the most part, but a frenzied desire to save self. Nothing but a system of discipline can prevent the weak from being sacrificed to the strong.

There was just so much discipline on board, that the Captain's roaring order to call up the women and children was attended to. They were wailing as they were hustled into the boat. No mother set her foot in it until every child belonging to her had been tumbled in before her. Wives were in a sad pass. They clutched at their husbands and smuggled them into the boat at the risk of upsetting it.

Just as it was about to be pushed off, Mr. Grimwood's peremptory voice was raised high. "Stop a moment!" he called loudly; "another lady!"

At the instant of Miss Leighton's leaving him he put his small strong-box into her hands. She remembered afterwards that he had spoken quietly, but with wonderful quickness and clearness, as if these few last sentences were the outcome of a whole world of thought he had been fain to conceal. She seemed to read in his face that he looked for nothing but death after she had gone from him, and that as death only it would not be loathsome to him. She would have thought herself contemptible if at such a moment she had fettered her demonstrations by any apprehensions as to the after-construction that might be put upon them. She raised her face to his, put both her arms about his neck, and kissed him on the lips, as if in tearing her body away she was leaving her soul in his keeping. Then it was that he said what was on his mind.

"I can't help myself, darling! It's just as well that I should be going out of the world. We couldn't have made things square, I know! I only want you to remember that I would rather die like this than live as I did before I saw you."

If he had more to explain, there was no time for it.

The sad boat pushed off, and already a wild fight for the means of salvation was raging all round him. The cynic watched the little boat so long as it remained within sight. It was cheering to see it pass out from the ghastly red influence of the ugly flames, into the sweet gold-scattering light of the morning sun. When it was lost in the brightness of those wholesome beams, the apotheosis of the cynic had begun. Who will say he was to be pitied? A barren life is not such a boon that any, save the timorous, need cling to it. But it is worth living even through a barren life to know an instant's unalloyed happiness at the last. What if the happiness involve the surrender of all your finely-constructed theories?—if it prove that you have been blundering from the beginning? What if the discovery come too late for you individually? You could not have made such a discovery without incorporating yourself so far with humanity as to die Christ-like—hoping for all! For to know the rapture of merging your spiritual being into that of another is dimly to conceive the possibility of an after-fulness of content for all that part of your nature which is not entangled with the bodily mechanism. That is why—since materialists logically maintain that the heart is nothing more than a muscular viscus, and the brain a whitish viscus, and tell us that the dissolution of these two means the annihilation of the keenly-conscious self—we, being unable to gainsay in truth a single reason advanced by materialists, may find an aimless life atoned for by an unreasoning flash of hope at the last. No matter how it is brought about, to die while you are in possession of it is to rejoice that you were born. Who would refuse the alternative?

Perhaps Miss Leighton, finding the cynic's money heavy and cold compared with the cynic's love, wished in after-years that she had flung it into the boat and stayed behind herself, to share in a hope-crowned death. Perhaps the shadowy outline in the Plymouth harbour developed into a prosaic husband, who liked modern cooking better than Greek art. Perhaps his wife thought sometimes of a tranquil southern sea, all aglow with a lurid stain—a sea ready to take into mysterious depths of changing colour two tightly-locked bodies that should never have been separated. Perhaps she dreamed all this after a futile fashion of her own. It is one thing to poetise about going to the bottom of the sea when in a cheerful sitting-room with a bright fire, and another thing to be brought face to face with it on a flame-shrouded ship a hundred miles from land.

As for deciding whether the cynic's fate or the girl's was the better one—it is for each one to judge according to his lights.

A PHILANTHROPIST'S EXPERIMENT

I

Oh, suffering, sad humanity;
Oh, ye afflicted ones, who lie,
Steeped to the lips in misery.

Longfellow

It is necessary to obtain something of an insight into Mr. Boundy's character to arrive at an understanding of his experiment, its most distinctive feature being a tendency to act upon impulse, which, after all, is nothing more than the sudden provoking to action of a latent principle underlying the conventional considerations that rule our everyday lives. For, as regards the theory that generous impulses may spring from all orders of mind, I can no more believe that they can be evoked in certain narrow organisations than that a creature without an ear for music may be startled into melody. Mr. Boundy's impulses were the result of an under-current of kindly feeling for his fellow. Even a sixteen years' perfunctory fulfilment of magisterial duties in a decayed mining town in Victoria had not tinged this feeling with misanthropy. On the contrary, it endured through all the irksomeness of a daily contact with the victims of marital amenities and adulterated whisky; though it must be conceded that every time he took his seat upon the bench he did himself as great a violence as certain weak and well-meaning divines of the present day must do themselves every time they mount into the pulpit and deliver a discourse within the confines of strict orthodoxy—being hampered, in fact, by the possession of a bump that no judicative person, from Brutus downwards, should have been allowed to develop. Phrenologists have called such a bump the "organ of benevolence;" and allowing, in pursuance of their theory, a corresponding depression for every elevation, it is probable that, somewhere about the firm and combative regions, Mr. Boundy's head would have been found to exhibit dents instead of ridges.

This was especially observable in his illogical conclusions respecting life. For sixteen years he hardly ever passed a day without seeing some offshoot of corruption that all the prisons and fines in existence could not have restrained from following its bent—that to knock on the head would have been tantamount to uprooting a sort of human dock—and yet, from an extra-judicial point of view, he was fond of maintaining that every entity had what he called its "nook" in creation. That the "nook" of some of the smaller species of entity was more often than not inside the bodies of some of the larger, and that the "nook" of many a stalwart youth was occasionally within the trenches, were facts of a disagreeable prominence. But accidents of this nature might be interpreted as representing all that we are accustomed to call "Evil," and once looked at in the light of irregularities, accorded perfectly with Mr. Boundy's theory, and allowed him the full enjoyment of the optimism almost invariably consequent upon the possession of a bump of benevolence.

It was through this comfortable, self-involved medium that he made up his mind to see all the little inconsistencies incidental to even the highest phase of civilization—upon which Mr. Boundy was now about to enter—for he had served his probationary sixteen years, not in doing a sentence, but in passing sentences upon others, and the goal of all this uncongenial labour lay right before him in European travel. He could now exchange, for the miscellaneous row of stores and public-houses, most of which were only kept in existence by the topers who came before him with such confiding persistency, the colonnade of the Rue de Rivoli, and expend, maybe, a little genuine sentiment upon some of those grand achievements that have their archetype in Greek art, instead of bestowing servile admiration upon the new lodge (shaped like a large herring-tin) of the U.O.O. or the

U.O.R. of Burrumberie. It is a fact that he abased himself before the marvels of the old world with a zest hardly in accordance with the self-adjusting spirit of a naturalized Australian. For Mr. Boundy, despite the unwarrantable size of the afore-mentioned bump, had none of the gloomy philosophy whereby Dr. Young was led to a conclusion no better than that of many a *blasé* worldling respecting the futility of expending admiration or enthusiasm upon mere worldly objects. And, touching the bump, as it was evident that he could not possibly leave it behind him, nor even reconcile it in a reasonable way to a good many of the consequences resulting from overcrowded cities, he promised himself that he would keep it in subjection by adhering to his favourite theory, and remembering that evil, like dirt, was a sort of misplaced matter, and, in fact, would not be evil at all if it were not for the little mistake which had caused a confusion as to the "nooks" of a large proportion of beings.

Mr. Boundy, moreover, was not the first instance of a person (as well-intentioned as Don Quixote) whose faith in his own power of adjusting part of this confusion was sincere. Chance (which, with all due deference to South, I must here make use of in the "impious and profane signification" attributed to it by the heathen) was the sole cause that led Mr. Boundy to test his theory individually. For where could there have been a more unlikely place for finding any one in doubt as to his "nook" than the platform of the railway station known as the "Gare du Nord," just without Paris? Stern officialdom (French suspicion) would make you "suspect" if you showed any hesitancy as to your immediate destination. Even Mr. Boundy, whose fresh colonial colour and mild magisterial eyes might certainly have exonerated from the suspicion of any ferocious Bonapartist designs,[18] had an uncomfortable sense of being followed by watchful, beady eyes because he had stammered in the attempt to give too French a turn to the word called by general English consent "Boolong". Watched, too, even after it was evident that he was waiting in a deprecatory way for his train—which was late—and whiling away the time, without reference to politics, by curiously regarding the semaphore. Seen in the semi-light of a winter's afternoon, when a long conflict between the dethroned sun and the rising moon had occasioned a fantastic twilight, there was a fascination about its erratic movements that obliged him to watch it for a while. It was like a modern Briareus[19] or a gaunt pugilist—spasmodically jerking out its stiff arms in a sort of general challenge to the world. All modern appliances are marvels for the uninitiated. Mr. Boundy might have pondered long on the pugilistic attitude of the semaphore but for an event that, while he was most intent upon it, aimed a sudden thrust at his bump and his theory all at the same time. And what was the thrust that struck home with such force! Nothing but the sound of two meaningless words, "Maman! Maman!" that Mr. Boundy had assuredly heard over and over again from the benches along the Champs Elysées without much disturbance to his bachelor's heart thereby. But these tones were nasalised by suffering. They were reiterated in a voice of cracked intensity, at once imperious and weak. They might have come from the wheezy lungs of an octogenarian, as well as from those of a worn infant, but, wherever they had come from, only hunger could have lent them a ring so persistently feeble and clamorous. They broke in upon Mr. Boundy's speculative meditations like the intermittent wail of a curlew, an intrusion of the spirit of want and disquiet upon a mind inclined to see only the agreeable surface of things, to the point even of carrying an unpleasant promise of repeating themselves with importunate distinctness next time he might find occasion to discourse upon "nooks"; for here was a being that could hardly have had a responsible voice in the selection of its "nook", yet was held accountable, as Mr. Boundy inferred from the sort of despairing protest that sounded through the monotonous cry, "Maman! Maman!" And, strangely enough, no one seemed to heed the appeal! Least of all the

"Maman" appealed to, who, with the child in her arms, bound up in the same flimsy shawl that covered her own shoulders, displayed all the apathy of the unjust judge under somewhat similar circumstances. Our philanthropist moved a little closer to her. It seemed to him that her eyes were fixed with covetous longing upon a golden-wigged, red-lipped, beautifully-formed woman, who, in rich travelling dress, had apparently found her "nook" in a *coupé*, which she shared with a sensual-lipped old gentleman.

She herself, seen through the mist of the gathering winter evening, by the sort of illusory gas rays that brought into prominence only the upper part of her body, reminded Mr. Boundy of the ancient image of Night, holding in her arms the twin children Sleep and Death. For though only one of these might be said to be actually present, Mr. Boundy could not fail to perceive that the other would creep quietly into its place if he did not upon this occasion make good his theory, that for every existence there is, somewhere or other, its corresponding "nook".

I cannot say that it discomposed him excessively to find that his French was more at his command in the free translation of a treatise by Montesquieu than in the following of Parisian *argot*, "since all mankind's concern is charity." Rosalie—Rosalies, by the way, are as plentiful in Paris as Sarah Anns in London—jerked her child into a momentary suspension of its weak breath, transforming the dreary "Maman! Maman!" into a subdued bleat, and fixed her hard, bright eyes upon Mr. Boundy with instant comprehension of his benevolent designs. She was by no means an impersonation of the peace-giving, spirit-soothing night of the ancients, when darkness signified repose for plant and animal, for faun and dryad, but more an outcome of all that is ignoble in the present restless night of the moderns, a production of gas and the *coulisses* of a theatre, rather than that of starlight and the leafy avenues of an arcadian forest. There was effrontery in every pinched feature of her cat-like face, effrontery in the seasoned weather-beaten hue of her sallow skin. It was clear that her "nook" was as yet unfound. Now, as Mr. Boundy had full confidence in his capability of finding it, herein lies his renowned experiment.

Still, as it might have proved rather embarrassing to give there and then, in a foreign tongue, the exact rendering of the special meaning he attached to the word "nook", and to expound to Rosalie the paramount importance of its fitness to the individual, he contented himself with pointing pityingly to the complaining child. Rosalie seized upon the cue afforded her to nod her head, directed a bony forefinger towards the child's mouth and her own, and shrugged her shoulders despairingly. It was as explicit as the gesture of the man Friday. Mr. Boundy responding by a feint of devouring a Barmecides' Feast,[20] with much smacking of the lips, invited Rosalie to share in it by slapping his trousers-pocket. She signified her willing alacrity by pointing in the direction of Paris and uttering a short chuckle full of meaning. Moreover, while Mr. Boundy resignedly took up his small valise, resolved to forego his trip to Boulogne, and inwardly quailing at the thought of having to run the gauntlet of the beaky-nosed officials, she found occasion to bestow a sharp pinch upon her exhausted child and wake it anew to the dreary refrain of "Maman! Maman!"

I wish I could say of my philanthropist, that, conscious of the innocence of his motives, he boldly demanded back his ticket-money. For I am aware that he looked the very image of deprecating guilt as he stole from the platform with Rosalie in his wake. What she was doing there has never been made clear, even to Mr. Boundy's satisfaction, unless, indeed, the cry of "Maman! Maman!" had so worked upon her unmaternal heart, that she was waiting an opportunity to thrust the child under the seats of one of the carriages. In which she would only have been following the example of a teacher regarded by her nation as the apostle of nature and humanity. Rousseau could discourse like an angel upon parental duties, and carry his babies at dead of night to a foundling hospital. Instinct, after all, is not a thing to be instilled or talked down. But Mr. Boundy would have said the mistake all arose because a father's "nook" was inappropriate in the instance of Rousseau.

There are modest little buildings known as *crémeries* in all the less magnificent streets of Paris—a kind of breakfast restaurant—where the bestowal of two sous upon the waiter in attendance will stamp you as a customer of high consideration. Rosalie was quick to detect the first of these before she had tramped past many corners by Mr. Boundy's side. Neither, it must be allowed, had made much progress, so far, in a conversational sense. Mr. Boundy, by way of considerately implying that she was in need of help, had queried, "Vous avez du besoin?"—whereat she had nodded in a sort of mystified acquiescence.

"De quoi?" Mr. Boundy had pursued, charmed with the facility with which he could speak French.

"Dame! de tout!" replied Rosalie, promptly, which sounded so like an English oath, that Mr. Boundy was at a loss how to respond.

On entering the *crémerie* the philanthropist quickly perceived that he was not entertaining "an angel unawares." Rosalie threw herself down in a chair near the stove, and gave her order for a "*biftek saignant*"—which order was echoed with a dreary prolongation of the word "*saigna-n-t*" down a flight of steps at the rear—as if the delight of being insolent were a part of the treat. She unstrapped the child from the shawl and set it on the sanded floor at her feet, indifferent as to its inability to stand. Mr. Boundy, having drawn from his experience of Australian police-courts the deduction that all children, even the children of beaten wives, were similarly round and fat and dirty, regarded Rosalie's peaky child with horror. For the first time he felt inclined to question whether it would not have been better, so far, without a "nook" at all, than a "nook" that could have misshapen childhood thus—leaving it as devoid of sex or age or humanity as a changeling. He could fancy its dwindling down into nothing but the dreary night-voice that had first attacked his philanthropic susceptibilities. But he was more inclined to accord it substantiality as soon as he saw it eat with a famished mien, clutching at the strips of *"bifteks saignant"* that Rosalie dropped into its lap, and gnawing them with its carnivorous little jaws, like a starved Abyssinian. When the pair had regaled themselves until even the greasily-golden slices of *"pommes frites"* fell from between their thin fingers, Mr. Boundy paid the score, and confirmed the waiter's opinion that he was an eccentric millionaire by giving him fivepence for himself. As for Rosalie, she scraped up the dregs of her coffee, picked up her satiated child, and followed Mr. Boundy out of the *crémerie*.

II

Thought he, this is the lucky hour,
Wines work when vines are in the flower;
This crisis then I will set my rest on,
And put her boldly to the question.

Butler

Rosalie's "mansarde", from a philanthropical point of view, was hardly a more eligible "nook" than the platform of the railway station. Misery in London grovels in the basement, in Paris it is perched on the housetops; inversely to the actual elevation is the ratio of the scale of well-being. Perhaps the brazen spirit that glittered in Rosalie's unwomanly eyes would have found less place there if she had not been suffered, night after night, to carry her starveling up the treadmill round of steep back-stairs, past the doors of eight kitchens, through the mingled steams of eight different kinds of soup; so Mr. Boundy reflected, at least, as he landed panting on the last step of all, and realised as a fact that this dark, impure corner was the type of the "nook" (materially, not figuratively, speaking) of perhaps some hundreds of thousands of beings.

As it was handsomely furnished with the remnants of a checked mattress and an old broom, Mr. Boundy felt some delicacy about inviting himself to take a seat. Standing, it was difficult to retain his usual magisterial dignity. But it was standing, nevertheless, while Rosalie sat like a Maori on her mattress, with her callous face turned up to his, that he gravely set about inaugurating his experiment.

And first, in such French as he could muster.

"What brought you to this plight?"

"Ask it of the patron! All is so dear since the war. I have been ill. I make my five sous the hour. It is not enough."

"Where is your husband?"

A quick glance of suspicion from the hardened eyes, and a laugh.

"Where, at least, is the father of your child?"

Another sharp glance and a shrug.

There is nothing the shrug proper does not convey from a French pair of shoulders. Thus—

"Will it be fine?" A shrug of doubt.

"You like that picture?" A shrug of dissent.

"Who spilt the ink?" A shrug of disavowal.

"A thousand thanks!" A shrug of deprecation.

"How shall we spend the afternoon?" A shrug of the completest deference to the inclinations of the proposer.

Rosalie's shrug might have meant anything, from negation of a husband's existence to indifference as to his whereabouts. Mr. Boundy concluded that the marital nook was as yet unfilled.

"I see you have got into the wrong place," he said, benignly. "There is a right place for every one who is born in the world; yours is right away from here. Tell me, would you like to live in a country where you would have plenty to eat and drink?"

"I hold not to leave Paris" (promptly).

"Eh! What! Not leave Paris!" exclaimed Mr. Boundy, much perplexed. He looked round upon the vermin-stained walls, exuding their stale odour of damp and dirt. As he passed, an echo of the never-dying clamour below faintly reached his hearing. He vaguely comprehended that Rosalie breathed in with the heavily-charged atmosphere a something intoxicating which she was very unwilling to leave—a whiff of the mingled mass of emanations, tangible and spiritual, that are ever mounting upwards from a great city, like a cloud of human incense. And still he could not, with his well-defined bump of benevolence, and a self-evolved theory almost rivalling that of Dr. Pangloss,[21] bring himself to believe that there are human beings that cling to the dust of great centres, like those unwholesome larvae that thrive in odorous chests upon the fibrous shreds of rich brocades, but would waste and fall into nothingness before the sunlight and the wide air without. "But you will die of want in Paris. Your child will die of want. It is only by a mistake that you are not accountable for that you come to be here. I can set it all right, however." Mr. Boundy parenthetically murmured in his own language something with reference to a "a million unoccupied nooks in the antipodes." "But you must consent to leave Paris."

"I do not care to live in the provinces."

As a philanthropist who had chanced upon a restive subject for an experiment that tended towards the enlightenment of humanity as to its destiny, there is something to be said in extenuation of Mr. Boundy's irritation. "You are a fool!" he said in very plain French. "I speak not of the provinces, but of a country far across the sea, where, if you work for a few hours every day, you and your child may have '*bifteks saignant*' twenty times in a week."

It was a searching appeal. What was there to counteract it save the deadened echo of the sounding life below, of which Rosalie's share displayed itself, partly in the wizened child, partly in her own shrivelled skin and hungry, unabashed eyes?

"Ribands, too, are cheap and abundant out there," added Mr. Boundy, in a musing tone of voice.

The echo of the fascination of Parisian life to even this one of its dreariest scapegoats was thus finally hushed. Surely a land of unlimited underdone beef-steaks and plenty of ribands must offer something of an equivalent for the loss of the vicarious joys of treading on the borders of an enchanted region. Though who can limit the extension of its spell? The Peri[22] might have been disporting herself in spice-laden breezes when she chose to cry before the entrance of heaven after a very derogatory fashion. Rosalie was more like a smooth-faced ape than a Peri, and Paris, in her case, was but a "fool's paradise" at the best. Yet, granting that such questions are purely relative, I doubt whether, even if no prospect of entering by the celestial gate had been held out to the Peri, she would not have preferred waiting her chance of catching some more stray gleams of "light upon her wings" to taking to respectable vagrancy among the grosser planets, at the bidding of a philanthropic and well-intentioned angel of Mr. Boundy's way of thinking.

III

He tried the luxury of doing good.

Crabbe

That faint flavour of magisterial pomposity, which the surmised suspicion of impertinent French officals had so completely taken out of Mr. Boundy, returned in full force when he again found himself outside the court-house of Burrumberie. It was further heightened by something of a "Sir Oracle" mien, as he walked erect down the street, called—in deference to the branching bush roads shadowed forth in its neighbourhood—Main Street. Main Street itself, of immense scope and width, was a mournful evidence of ambition and collapse. Its pavements were still in an embryo stage, allowing full facilities for the social intercourse of the goats and geese that represented the active, unconventional life of Burrumberie. The immense gaps between its low wooden buildings carried unpleasant suggestions of toothless jaws. In the distance were deserted shafts, and trees that had become mummified in the baked soil. It was necessary to glance at the far-away horizon, which will form as golden a background for gibbet as for arch of triumph, to remember that Burrumberie was of a piece with the world Mr. Boundy had so lately seen.

I have alluded to his oracular deportment, and must admit that, in a philanthropist, his elation was pardonable. A year ago, under a misty winter's sky, right in the heart of a clamorous throng, he had distinguished the dreary plaints of one of those entities whose minimum of superfluity helps to make up the sum of unexplained evil. And thereupon he had found an immediate outlet for the working of his theory. Long ago he had been inspired to feel that on the proper portioning out of "nooks" depended the well-being of humanity. Now he felt himself capable of illustrating his theory—of "speaking aloud for future times to hear"—

of recounting how an utterly stranded waif, transported to her appropriate "nook"—signifying thereby the nook Mr. Boundy had found for her—became forthwith a very model of industry and virtue. He could not fail to approve his own sagacity in the ensuring of this end.

For, bearing in mind Rosalie's carnivorous proclivities, how fitting it was that she should be received into the bosom of the butcher's family at the corner. A family, too, whose sanguineous hue was a complete advertisement in itself.

Mr. Boundy's benevolence had the first foretaste of its rapture when he stumbled over a bloated baby on the step— a baby that could no more in its present plethoric condition have concentrated the wail of superfluous humanity in its fretful cry than it could have awed and appalled Mr. Boundy into foregoing a journey for the sake of appeasing it.

"Now this is what I like!" said the philanthropist aloud, either with reference to tumbling over the baby or in approbation of its solidity; "you'll fill a big 'nook' one of these days, I can see! Where's Maman?"

"Maman! maman!" echoed the baby, in a sort of burlesque of its old professional cry.

"That's right," said Mr. Boundy, delighted, "and 'bif-tek' too. I thought as much!"

He turned into the shop. The butcher, whose mottled skin might have put his own sausages to the blush, held out his hand to the magistrate heartily. He had never had justice dealt to him during all Mr. Boundy's term of office, and he had served him with meat ever since the beginning of that time. This was quite enough in Burrumberie to establish an equality. "And how about my *protégée*?" asked Mr. Boundy beamingly, after he had carefully inquired into the well-being of Mrs. Butcher and the smaller butchers.

There was a suffusion in the butcher's mottled cheeks.

"It's this way, Mr. Boundy," he explained. "Your prodigy's give you what I should call leg-bail."

"Good gracious!" said Mr. Boundy. "But you know where she is, I hope."

"No, faith! she's give us the slip," said the butcher. "You meant well by her, I make no doubt of it, Mr. Boundy; but you didn't study the make of her. There wasn't no taming her. She put me in mind of a native cat one o' my little chaps had a fancy for rearing. Petting! Why, all the petting in the world wouldn't a' kept it from fretting its life away."

"But what did she want?" urged the philanthropist, with a sense that to be dictated to by the butcher did not exactly compensate for the astonishing miscarriage of his plan. "I found her in a sink of misery. What did she want beyond meat and drink, and a home for herself and her child?"

"That's where it is," said the butcher, meditatively; "it beats me, I tell you. But I see from the first she wouldn't settle down to it, and one day a French swagman must needs come into the shop, and there was a jabbering in their own tongue—I couldn't make head nor tale of it. I think I got hold o' them two words, though—'movement' and 'Paris'—for she was always harping on them in her outlandish way; and next day she was gone, and left the child behind her."

Gone, as Mr. Boundy afterwards found, without leaving a clue or a trace whereby to recapture her; gone, to carry out the blind design of sharing a stow-away's nook with the rats on some homeward-bound vessel; gone, to re-enter the shadows whence he had dragged her into the light, following, by an instinct that set his theory at derision, her entozooic destiny in the corrupt heart of Paris.[23]

And yet, as the magistrate passed again up the street, endeavouring to look through Rosalie's restless eyes at the stagnant life around him, he fell to thinking whether, through the ingratitude, the unmotherliness, the abandonment, there was a spark of some blind groping after progress in the impulse that led her to run away. It was not solely because cold is so cruel to the perceptions of an Italian that Dante made imprisonment in the ice the final and crowning anguish of the arch-offenders of mankind. The horror lay in the infinite stagnation it implied. Compared with this, the perpetual capering of the less guilty souls among pellets of flame was life and hope. Rosalie must needs find the "nook" before long that there can be no mistake about all of us filling sooner or later, and she would find it probably through the gates of the Hôtel Dieu, but was Mr. Boundy to relinquish his theory because he had chanced upon an exception? There cannot be, he told himself, a more ungrateful subject for experiment than a human organisation—or a more unsatisfactory one. For whereas, under vivisection, dogs or rabbits or frogs have the grace to do just what is expected of them, and as animals generally so comport themselves as to allow us to say, inclusive of all types, "The ass is stubborn; the dog is faithful; the horse is a noble, useful beast," and so on—of man it can only be said, with Dryden, that he "is always in the wrong."

And in such sweeping conclusion resulted our philanthropist's experiment. He found a temporary "nook", nevertheless, for Rosalie's child in his own household. It is known in the township as "Boundy's babby," and unless it dies of apoplexy, may yet vindicate his theory, about which he has had less to say latterly than before his foreign travels.

MONSIEUR CALOCHE

I

A more un-English, uncolonial appearance had never brightened the prosaic interior of Bogg & Company's big warehouse in Flinders Lane. Monsieur Caloche, waiting in the outer office, under fire of a row of curious eyes, was a wondrous study of "Frenchiness" to the clerks. His vivacious dark eyes, shining out of his sallow face, scarred and seamed by the marks of small-pox, met their inquisitive gaze with an expression that seemed to plead for leniency. The diabolical disease that had scratched the freshness from his face had apparently twisted some of the youthfulness out of it as well; otherwise it was only a young soul that could have been made so diffident by the consciousness that its habitation was disfigured. Some pains had been taken to obviate the effects of the disfigurement and to bring into prominence the smooth flesh that had been spared. It was not chance that had left exposed a round white throat, guiltless of the masculine Adam's apple, or that had brushed the fine soft hair, ruddily dark in hue like the eyes, away from a vein-streaked temple. A youth of unmanly susceptibilities, perhaps—but inviting sympathy rather than scorn—sitting patiently through the dreary silent three-quarters of an hour, with his back to the wall which separated him from the great head of the firm of Bogg & Co.

The softer-hearted of the clerks commiserated him. They would have liked to show their goodwill, after their own fashion, by inviting him to have a "drink", but—the possibility of shouting for a young Frenchman, waiting for an interview with their chief! . . . Any one knowing Bogg, of Bogg & Co., must have divined the outrageous absurdity of the notion. It was safer to suppose that the foreigner would have refused the politeness. He did not look as though whisky and water were as familiar to him as a tumbler of *eau sucrée*. The clerks had heard that it was customary in France to drink absinthe. Possibly the slender youth in his loose-fitting French paletôt reaching to his knees, and sitting easily upon shoulders that would have graced a shawl, had drunk deeply of this fatal spirit. It invested him with something mysterious in the estimation of the juniors, peering for traces of dissipation in his foreign face. But they could find nothing to betray it in the soft eyes, undimmed by the enemy's hand, or the smooth lips set closely over the even row of small French teeth. Monsieur Caloche lacked the happy French confidence which has so often turned a joke at the foot of the guillotine. His lips twitched every time the door of the private office creaked. It was a ground-glass door to the left of him, and as he sat, with his turned-up hat in his hand, patiently waiting, the clerks could see a sort of suppression overspreading his disfigured cheeks whenever the noise was repeated. It appeared that he was diffident about the interview. His credentials were already in the hands of the head of the firm, but no summons had come. His letter of recommendation, sent in fully half an hour back, stated that he was capable of undertaking foreign correspondence; that he was favourably known to the house of business in Paris whose principal had given him his letter of presentation; that he had some slight knowledge of the English language; that he had already given promise of distinguishing himself as an *homme de lettres*. This final clause of the letter was responsible for the length of time Monsieur Caloche was kept waiting. *Homme de lettres!* It was a stigma that Bogg, of Bogg and Co., could not overlook. As a practical man, a self-made man, a man who had opened up new blocks of country and imported pure stock into Victoria—what could be expected of him in the way of holding out a helping hand to a scribbler—a pauper who had spent his days in making rhymes in his foreign jargon? Bogg would have put your needy professionals into irons. He forgave no authors, artists, or actors who were not successful. *Homme de lettres!* Coupled with his poverty it was more unpardonable a title than jail-bird. There was nothing to prove that the latter title would not have fitted Monsieur Caloche as well. He was probably a ruffianly Communist.[24] The French Government could not get hold of all the rebels, and here was one in the outer office of Bogg & Co. coolly waiting for a situation.

Not so coolly, perhaps, as Bogg, in his aggrieved state of mind, was ready to conclude. For the day was a hot-wind day, and Bogg himself, in white waistcoat and dust-coat, sitting in the cool depths of his revolving-chair in front of the desk in his private office, was hardly aware of the driving dust and smarting grit emptied by shovelfuls upon the unhappy people without. He perspired, it is true, in deference to the state of his big thermometer, which even here stood above 85° in the corner, but having come straight from Brighton in his private brougham, he could wipe his moist bald head without besmearing his silk handkerchief with street grime. And it was something to be sitting here, in a lofty office, smelling of yellow soap and beeswax, when outside a north wind was tormenting the world with its puffs of hot air and twirling relays of baked rubbish and dirt. It was something to be surrounded by polished mahogany, cool to the touch, and cold iron safes, and maps that conveyed in their rippling lines of snowy undulations far-away suggestions of chill heights and mountain breezes. It was something to have iced water in the decanter at hand, and a little fountain opposite, gurgling a running reminder of babbling brooks dribbling through fern-tree valleys and wattle-studded flats. Contrasting the shaded coolness of the private office with the heat and turmoil without, there was no cause to complain.

Yet Bogg clearly had a grievance, written in the sour lines of his mouth, never too amiably expanded at the best of times, and his small, contracted eyes, full of shrewd suspicion-darting light. He read the letter sent in by Monsieur Caloche with the plentiful assistance of the tip of his broad forefinger, after a way peculiar to his early days, before he had acquired riches, or knighthood, or rotundity.

For Bogg, now Sir Matthew Bogg, of Bogg and Company, was a self-made man, in the sense that money makes the man, and that he had made the money before it could by any possibility make him. Made it by dropping it into his till in those good old times when all Victorian storekeepers were so many Midases, who saw their spirits and flour turn into gold under their handling; made it by pocketing something like three thousand per cent. upon every penny invested in divers blocks of scrubby soil hereafter to be covered by those grand and gloomy bluestone buildings which make of Melbourne a city of mourning; made it by reaching out after it, and holding fast to it, whenever it was within spirit-call or finger-clutch, from his early grog-shanty days, when he detected it in the dry lips of every grimy digger on the flat, to his latter station-holding days, when he sniffed it in the drought which brought his neighbours low. Add to which he was lucky—by virtue of a certain inherent faculty he possessed in common with the Vanderbilts, the Stewarts, the Rothschilds of mankind—and far-seeing. He could forestall the news in the *Mark Lane Express*. He was almost clairvoyant in the matter of rises in wool. His luck, his foresight, were only on a par with his industry, and the end of all his slaving and sagacity was to give him at sixty years of age a liver, a paunch, an income bordering on a hundred thousand pounds, and the title of Sir Matthew Bogg.

It was known that Sir Matthew had worked his way to the colonies, acting indiscriminately as pig-sticker and deck-swabber on board the *Sarah Jane*. In his liverless, paunchless, and titleless days he had tossed for coppers with the flat-footed sailors on the forecastle. Now he was bank director, railway director, and a number of other things that formed a graceful flourish after Sir Matthew, but that would have sounded less euphonious in the wake of plain "Bogg." Yet "plain Bogg" Nature had turned him out, and "plain Bogg" he would always remain while in the earthly possession of

his round, overheated face and long, irregular teeth. His hair
had abandoned its lawful territory on the top of his head,
and planted itself in a vagrant fashion, in small tufts in
his ears and nostrils. His eyebrows had run riot over his
eyes, but his eyes asserted themselves through all. They were
eyes that, without being stronger or larger or bolder than
any average pair of eyes to be met with in walking down
the street, had such a knack of "taking your measure" that
no one could look at them without discomfiture. In the
darkened atmosphere of the Flinders Lane office, Sir Matthew
knew how to turn these colourless unwinking orbs to account.
To the maliciously inclined among the clerks in the outer
office there was nothing more amusing than the crestfallen
appearance of the applicants, as they came out by the ground-
glass door, compared with the jauntiness of their entrance.
Young men who wanted colonial experience, overseers who
applied for managerships on his stations, youths fresh from
school who had a turn for the bush, had all had specimens
of Sir Matthew's mode of dealing with his underlings. But
his favourite plan, his special hobby, was to "drop on to
them unawares."

There is nothing in the world that gives such a zest to
life as the possession of a hobby, and the power of indulging
it. We may be pretty certain that the active old lady's white
horse at Banbury Cross was nothing more than a hobby-
horse, as soon as we find out in the sequel that she "had
rings on her fingers and bells on her toes," and that "she
shall have music wherever she goes." It is the only horse
an old lady could be perpetually engaged in riding without
coming to grief—the only horse that ever makes us travel
through life to the sound of music wherever we go.

From the days when Bogg had the merest shred of humanity
to bully, in the shape of a waif from the Chinese camp,
the minutes slipped by with a symphony they had never
possessed before. As fulness of time brought him increase
of riches and power, he yearned to extend the terror of his
sway. It was long before he tasted the full sweetness of making

strong men tremble in their boots. Now, at nearly sixty years
of age, he knew all the delights of seeing victims, sturdier
and poorer than himself, drop their eyelids before his gaze.
He was aware that the men in the yard cleared out of his
path as he walked through it; that his managers up-country
addressed him in tones of husky conciliation; that every eye
met his with an air of deprecation, as much as to apologise
for the fact of existing in his presence; and in his inner-
most heart he believed that in the way of mental sensation
there could be nothing left to desire. But how convey the
impression of rainbow-tints to eyes that have never opened
upon aught save universal blackness? Sir Matthew had never
seen an eye brighten, a small foot dance, at his approach.
A glance of impotent defiance was the only equivalent he
knew for a gleam of humid affection. He was accustomed
to encounter a shifting gaze. The lowest form of self-interest
was the tie which bound his people to him. He paid them
as butts, in addition to paying them as servants. Where would
have been his daily appetiser in the middle of the day if
there had been no yard, full of regulations impossible to
obey; no warehouse to echo his harsh words of fault-finding;
no servile men, and slouching fast-expanding boys, to scuttle
behind the big cases, or come forth as if they were being
dragged by hooks, to stand with sheepish expression before
him? And when he had talked himself hoarse in town, where
would have been the zest of wandering over his stations,
of surveying his fat bullocks and woolly merinos, if there
had been no accommodating managers to listen reverentially
to his loudly-given orders, and take with dejected, apologetic
air his continued rating? The savour of life would have
departed,—not with the bodily comfort and the consequence
that riches bring, but with the power they confer of asserting
yourself before your fellow-men after any fashion you please.
Bogg's fashion was to bully them, and he bullied them
accordingly.

But, you see, Monsieur Caloche is still waiting; in the
position, as the junior clerks are well aware, of the confiding

calf awaiting butchery in a frolicsome mood outside the butcher's shop. Not that I would imply that Monsieur Caloche frolicked, even metaphorically speaking. He sat patiently on with a sort of sad abstracted air; unconsciously pleating and unpleating the brim of his soft Paris hat, with long lissome fingers that might have broidered the finest silk on other than male hands. The flush of colour, the slight trembling of lips, whenever there was a noise from within, were the only signs that betrayed how acutely he was listening for a summons. Despite the indentations that had marred for ever the smoothness of the face, and pitted the forehead and cheeks as if white gravel had been shot into them, the colour that came and went so suddenly was pink as rose-coloured lake. It stained even the smooth white neck and chin, upon which the faintest traces of down were not yet visible to the scrutinising eyes of the juniors.

Outside, the north wind ran riot along the pavement, upsetting all orderly arrangements for the day with dreadful noise and fussiness, battering trimly-dressed people into red-eyed wretches heaped up with dust; wrenching umbrellas from their handles, and blinding their possessors trying to run after them; filling open mouths with grit, making havoc with people's hats and tempers, and proving itself as great a blusterer in its character of a peppery emigrant as in its original *rôle* of the chilly Boreas of antiquity.

Monsieur Caloche had carefully wiped away from his white wristband the dust that it had driven into his sleeve, and now the dust on his boots—palpably large for the mere slips of feet they enclosed—seemed to give him uneasiness; but it would seem that he lacked the hardihood to stoop and flick it away. When, finally, he extended surreptitiously a timid hand, it might have been observed of his uncovered wrist that it was singularly frail and slender. This delicacy of formation was noticeable in every exterior point. His small white ear, setting close to his head, might have been wrapped up over and over again in one of the fleshy lobes that stretched away from Sir Matthew's skull. Decidedly, the two men

101

were of a different order of species. One was a heavy mastiff of lupine tendencies—the other a delicate Italian greyhound, silky, timorous, quivering with sensibility.

And there had been time for the greyhound to shiver long with expectancy before the mastiff prepared to swallow him up.

It was a quarter to twelve by the gloomy-faced clock in the outer office, a quarter to twelve by all the clerks' watches, adjusted every morning to the patriarch clock with unquestioning faith, when Monsieur Caloche had diffidently seated himself on the chair in the vicinity of the ground-glass door. It was half-past twelve by the gloomy-faced clock, half-past twelve by all the little watches that toadied to it, when Sir Matthew's bell rang. It was a bell that must have inherited the spirit of a fire-bell or a doctor's night-bell. It had never been shaken by Sir Matthew's fingers without causing a fluttering in the outer office. No one knew what hair-suspended sword might be about to fall on his head before the messenger returned. Monsieur Caloche heard it ring, sharply and clamorously, and raised his head. The white-faced messenger, returning from his answer to the summons, and speaking with the suspension of breath that usually afflicted him after an interview with Sir Matthew, announced that "Mister Caloosh" was wanted, and diving into the gloomy recess in the outer office, relapsed into his normal occupation of breathing on his penknife and rubbing it on his sleeve.

Monsieur Caloche meanwhile stood erect, more like the startled greyhound than ever. To the watchful eyes of the clerks, staring their full at his retreating figure, he seemed to glide rather than step through the doorway. The ground-glass door, attached by a spring from the inside, shut swiftly upon him, as if it were catching him in a trap, and so hid him in full from their curious scrutiny. For the rest, they could only surmise. The lamb had given itself up to the butcher's knife. The diminutive greyhound was in the mastiff's grip.

Would the knife descend on the instant? Would the mastiff fall at once upon the trembling foreigner, advancing with sleek uncovered head, and hat held in front by two quivering hands? Sir Matthew's usual glare of reception was more ardent than of custom as Monsieur Caloche approached. If every "foreign adventurer" supposed he might come and loaf upon Bogg, of Bogg & Company, because he was backed up by a letter from a respectable firm, Sir Matthew would soon let him find out he was mistaken! His glare intensified as the adventurous stripling glided with softest footfall to the very table where he was sitting, and stood exactly opposite to him. None so adventurous, however, but that his lips were white and his bloodless face a pitiful set-off to the cruelly prominent marks that disfigured it. There was a terror in Monsieur Caloche's expression apart from the awe inspired by Sir Matthew's glare which might have disarmed a butcher or even a mastiff. His large, soft eyes seemed to ache with repressed tears. They pleaded for him in a language more convincing than words, "I am friendless—I am a stranger—I am—" but no matter! They cried out for sympathy and protection, mutely and unconsciously.

But to Sir Matthew's perceptions visible terror had only one interpretation. It remained for him to "find out" Monsieur Caloche. He would "drop on to him unawares" one of these days. He patted his hobby on the back, seeing a gratification for it in prospective, and entering shortly upon his customary stock of searching questions, incited his victim to reply cheerfully and promptly by looking him up and down with a frown of suspicion.

"What brought you 'ere?"

"Please?" said Monsieur Caloche, anxiously.

He had studied a vocabulary opening with "Good-day, sir. What can I have the pleasure of doing for you this morning?" The rejoinder to which did not seem to fit in with Sir Matthew's special form of inquiry.

"What brought you 'ere, I say?" reiterated Sir Matthew, in a roar, as if deafness were the only impediment on the

part of foreigners in general to a clear comprehension of
our language.

"De sheep, Monsieur! La Reine Dorée," replied Monsieur
Caloche, in low-toned, guttural, musical French.

"That ain't it," said Sir Matthew, scornfully. "What did
you come 'ere for? What are you fit for? What can you do?"

Monsieur Caloche raised his plaintive eyes. His sad
desolation was welling out of their inmost depths. He had
surmounted the first emotion that had driven the blood to
his heart at the outset, and the returning colour, softening
the seams and scars in his cheeks, gave him a boyish bloom.
It deepened as he answered with humility, "I will do what
Monsieur will! I will do my possible!"

"I'll soon see how you shape," said Sir Matthew, irritated
with himself for the apparent difficulty of thoroughly bullying
the defenceless stranger. "I don't want any of your parley-
vooing in my office—do you hear! I'll find you work—
jolly quick, I can tell you! Can you mind sheep? Can you
drive bullocks, eh? Can you put up a post and rail? You
ain't worth your salt if you can't use your 'ands!"

He cast such a glance of withering contempt on the tapering
white fingers with olive-shaped nails in front of him that
Monsieur Caloche instinctively sheltered them in his hat.
"Go and get your traps together! I'll find you a billet, never
fear!"

"*Mais, Monsieur*"—

"Go and get your traps together, I say! You can come
'ere again in an hour. I'll find you a job up-country!" His
peremptory gesture made any protest on the part of Monsieur
Caloche utterly unavailing. There was nothing for him to
do but to bow and to back in a bewildered way from the
room. If the more sharp-eared of the clerks had not been
in opportune contiguity to the ground-glass door during Sir
Matthew's closing sentences, Monsieur Caloche would have
gone away with the predominant impression that "Sir Bang"
was an *enragé*, who disapproved of salt with mutton and
beef, and was clamorous in his demands for "traps," which

Monsieur Caloche, with a gleam of enlightenment in the midst of his heart-sickness and perplexity, was proud to remember meant "an instrument for ensnaring animals." It was with a doubt he was too polite to express that he accepted the explanation tendered him by the clerks, and learned that if he "would strike while the iron is hot" he must come back in an hour's time with his portmanteau packed up. He was a lucky fellow, the juniors told him, to jump into a billet without any bother; they wished to the Lord they were in *his* shoes, and could be drafted off to the Bush at a moment's notice.

Perhaps it seemed to Monsieur Caloche that these congratulations were based on the Satanic philosophy of "making evil his good." But they brought with them a flavour of the human sympathy for which he was hungering. He bowed to the clerks all round before leaving, after the manner of a court-page in an opera. The hardiest of the juniors ran to the door after he was gone. Monsieur Caloche was trying to make head against the wind. The warm blast was bespattering his injured face. It seemed to revel in the pastime of filling it with grit. One small hand was spread in front of the eyes—the other was resolutely holding together the front of his long, light paletôt, which the rude wind had sportively thrown open. The junior was cheated of his fun. Somehow the sight did not strike him as being quite so funny as it ought to have been.

II

The station hands, in their own language, "gave Frenchy best." No difference of nationality could account for some of his eccentricities. As an instance, with the setting in of the darkness he regularly disappeared. It was supposed that he camped up a tree with the birds. The wit of the wool-shed surmised that "Froggy" slept with his relatives, and it would be found that he had "croaked" with them one of these odd times. Again, there were shearers ready to swear that he had "blubbered" on finding some sportive ticks on his neck. He was given odd jobs of wool-sorting to do, and was found to have a mania for washing the grease off his hands whenever there was an instant's respite. Another peculiarity was his aversion to blood. By some strange coincidence, he could never be found whenever there was any slaughtering on hand. The most plausible reason was always advanced for necessitating his presence in some far-distant part of the run. Equally he could never be induced to learn how to box—a favourite Sunday morning and summer evening pastime among the men. It seemed almost to hurt him when damage was done to one of the assembled noses. He would have been put down as a "cur" if it had not been for his pluck in the saddle, and for his gentle winning ways. His pluck, indeed, seemed all concentrated in his horse-manship. Employed as a boundary-rider, there was nothing he would not mount, and the station hands remarked, as a thing "that beats them once for all," that the "surliest devils" on the place hardly ever played up with him. He employed no arts. His bridle-hand was by no means strong. Yet it remained a matter of fact that the least amenable of horses generally carried him as if they liked to bear his weight. No one being sufficiently learned to advance the hypothesis of magnetism, it was concluded that he carried a charm.

This power of touch extended to human beings. It was

almost worth while spraining a joint or chopping at a finger to be bandaged by Monsieur Caloche's deft fingers. His horror of blood never stood in his way when there was a wound to be doctored. His supple hands, browned and strengthened by his outdoor work, had a tenderness and a delicacy in their way of going to work that made the sufferer feel soothed and half-healed by their contact. It was the same with his manipulation of things. There was a refinement in his disposition of the rough surroundings that made them look different after he had been among them.

And not understood, jeered at, petted, pitied alternately— with no confidant of more sympathetic comprehension than the horse he bestrode—was Monsieur Caloche absolutely miserable? Granting that it were so, there was no one to find it out. His brown eyes had such an habitually wistful expression, he might have been born with it. Very trifles brought a fleeting light into them—a reminiscence, perhaps that, while it crowned him with "sorrow's crown of sorrow," was yet a reflection of some past joy. He took refuge in his ignorance of the language directly he was questioned as to his bygone life. An embarrassed little shrug, half apologetic, but powerfully conclusive, was the only answer the most curious examiner could elicit.

It was perceived that he had a strong objection to looking in the glass, and invariably lowered his eyes on passing the cracked and uncompromising fragment of mirror supported on two nails against the planking that walled the rough, attached kitchen. So decided was this aversion that it was only when Bill, the blacksmith, asked him chaffingly for a lock of his hair that he perceived with confusion how wantonly his silken curls were rioting round his neck and temples. He cut them off on the spot, displaying the transparent skin beneath. Contrasted with the clear tan that had overspread his scarred cheeks and forehead, it was white as freshly-drawn milk.

He was set down on the whole as given to moping; but, taking him all round, the general sentiment was favourable to him. Possibly it was with some pitiful prompting of the sort that the working manager sent him out of the way one still morning, when Sir Matthew's buggy, creaking under the unwelcome preponderance of Sir Matthew himself, was discerned on its slow approach to the homestead. A most peaceful morning for the initiation of Sir Matthew's blustering presence! The sparse gum-leaves hung as motionless on their branches as if they were waiting to be photographed. Their shadows on the yellowing grass seemed painted into the soil. The sky was as tranquil as the plain below. The smoke from the homestead reared itself aloft in a long, thinly-drawn column of grey. A morning of heat and repose, when even the sunlight does not frolic and all nature toasts itself, quietly content. The dogs lay blinking at full length, their tails beating the earth with lazy, measured thump. The sheep seemed rooted to the patches of shade, apathetic as though no one wore flannel vests or ate mutton-chops. Only the mingled voices of wild birds and multitudinous insects were upraised in a blended monotony of subdued sounds. Not a morning to be devoted to toil! Rather, perchance, to a glimmering perception of a golden age, when sensation meant bliss more than pain, and to be was to enjoy.

But to the head of the firm of Bogg & Company, taking note of scattered thistles and straggling wire fencing, warmth and sunshine signified only dry weather. Dry weather clearly implied a fault somewhere, for which somebody must be called to account. Sir Matthew had the memory of a strategist. Underlying all considerations of shorthorns and merinos was the recollection of a timid foreign lad to be suspected for his shy, bewildered air—to be suspected again for his slim white hands—to be doubly suspected and utterly condemned for his graceful bearing, his appealing eyes, that even now Sir Matthew could see with their soft lashes drooping over them as he fronted them in his darkened office in Flinders Lane. A scapegoat for dry weather, for obtrusive thistles, for straggling fencing! A waif of foreign scum to be found out! Bogg had promised himself that he would "drop on him unawares." Physically, Bogg was carried over the ground by a fast trotter; spiritually, he was borne along on his hobby, ambling towards its promised gratification with airy speed.

The working manager, being probably of Bacon's way of thinking, that "dissimulation is but a faint kind of policy," did not, in his own words, entirely "knuckle down" to Sir Matthew. His name was Blunt—he was proud to say it— and he would show you he could make his name good if you "crossed" him. Yet Blunt could bear a good deal of "crossing" when it came to the point. Within certain limits, he concluded that the side on which his bread was buttered was worth keeping uppermost, at the cost of some hard words from his employer.

And he kept it carefully uppermost on this especial morning, when the quietude of the balmy atmosphere was broken by Sir Matthew's growls. The head of the firm, capturing his manager at the door of the homestead, had required him to mount into the double-seated buggy with him. Blunt reckoned that these tours of inspection in the companionship of Bogg were more conducive to taking off flesh than a week's hard training. He listened with docility, nevertheless, to plaints and ratings—was it not a fact that his yearly salaries had already made a nest-egg of large proportions?— and might have listened to the end, if an evil chance had not filled him with a sudden foreboding. For, pricking his way over the plain, after the manner of Spenser's knight, Monsieur Caloche, on a fleet, newly broken-in two-year-old, was riding towards them. Blunt could feel that Sir Matthew's eyes were sending out sparks of wrath. For the first time in his life he hazarded an uncalled-for opinion.

"He's a good working chap, that, sir!"—indicating by a jerk of the head that the lad now galloping across the turf was the subject of his remark.

"Ah!" said Sir Matthew.

It was all he said, but it was more than enough.

Blunt fidgeted uneasily. What power possessed the boy to make him show off his riding at this juncture? If he could have stopped him, or turned him back, or waved him off!—but his will was impotent.

Monsieur Caloche, well back in the saddle, his brown eyes shining, his disfigured face flushed and glowing, with wide felt-hat drawn closely over his smooth small head, with slender knees close pressed to the horse's flanks, came riding on, jumping small logs, bending with flexible joints under straggling branches, never pausing in his reckless course, until on a sudden he found himself almost in front of the buggy, and, reining up, was confronted in full by the savage gleam of Sir Matthew's eyes. It was with the old scared expression that he pulled off his wideawake and bared his head, black and silky as a young retriever's. Sir Matthew knew how to respond to the boy's greeting. He stood up in the buggy and shook his fist at him; his voice, hoarse from the work he had given it that morning, coming out with rasping intensity.

"What the devil do you mean by riding my 'orses' tails off, eh?"

Monsieur Caloche, in his confusion, straining to catch the full meaning of the question, looked fearfully round at the hind-quarters of the two-year-old, as if some hitherto unknown phenomenon peculiar to Australian horses might in fact have suddenly left them tailless.

But the tail was doing such good service against the flies at the moment of his observations, that, reassured, he turned his wistful gaze upon Sir Matthew.

"Monsieur," he began apologetically, "permit that I explain it to you. I did ga-lopp."

"You can ga-lopp to hell!" said Sir Matthew with furious mimicry. "I'll teach you to ruin my 'orses' legs!"

Blunt saw him lift his whip and strike Monsieur Caloche on the chest. The boy turned so unnaturally white that the manager looked to see him reel in his saddle. But he only swayed forward and slipped to the ground on his feet. Sir Matthew, sitting down again in the buggy with an uncomfortable sensation of some undue excess it might have been as well to recall, saw this white face for the flash of an instant's space, saw its desperation, its shame, its trembling lips; then he was aware that the two-year-old stood riderless in front of him, and away in the distance the figure of a lad was speeding through the timber, one hand held against his chest, his hat gone and he unheeding, palpably sobbing and crying in his loneliness and defencelessness as he stumbled blindly on.

Run-away boys, I fear, call forth very little solicitude in any heart but a mother's. A cat may be nine-lived, but a boy's life is centuple. He seems only to think it worth keeping after the best part of it is gone. Boys run away from schools, from offices, from stations, without exciting more than an ominous prognostication that they will go to the bad. According to Sir Matthew's inference, Monsieur Caloche had "gone to the bad" long ago—*ergo*, it was well to be rid of him. This being so, what utterly inconsistent crank had laid hold of the head of the great firm of Bogg & Company, and tortured him through a lengthy afternoon and everlasting night, with the vision of two despairing eyes and a scarred white face? Even his hobby cried out against him complainingly. It was not for this that it had borne him prancing along. Not to confront him night and day with eyes so distressful that he could see nothing else. Would it be always so? Would they shine mournfully out of the dim recesses of his gloomy office in Flinders Lane, as they shone here in the wild bush on all sides of him?—so relentlessly sad that it would have been a relief to see them change into the vindictive eyes of the Furies who gave chase to Orestes.[25] There was clearly only one remedy against such a fate, and that was to change the nature of the expression which haunted him by calling up another in its place. But how and when!

Sir Matthew prowled around the homestead the second morning after Monsieur Caloche's flight, in a manner unaccountable to himself. That he should return "possessed" to his elaborate warehouse, where he would be alone all day—and his house of magnificent desolation, where he would be alone all night, was fast becoming a matter of impossibility. What sums out of all proportion would he not have forfeited to have seen the white-faced foreign lad, and to be able to pay him out for the discomfort he was causing him—instead of being bothered by the sight of his "cursed belongings" at every turn! He could not go into the stable without seeing some of his gimcracks; when he went blustering into the kitchen it was to stumble over a pair of miniature boots, and a short curl of hair, in silken rings, fell off the ledge at his very feet. There was only one thing to be done! Consulting with Blunt, clumsily enough, for nothing short of desperation would have induced Sir Matthew to approach the topic of Monsieur Caloche, he learned that nothing had been seen or heard of the lad since the moment of his running away.

"And 'twasn't in the direction of the township, neither," added Blunt, gravely. "I doubt the sun'll have made him stupid, and he'll have camped down some place on the run."

Blunt's insinuation anent the sun was sheer artifice, for Blunt, in his private heart, did not endorse his own suggestion in the least degree. It was his belief that the lad had struck a shepherd's hut, and was keeping (with a show of common-sense he had not credited him with) out of the way of his savage employer. But it was worth while making use of the artifice to see Sir Matthew's ill-concealed uneasiness. Hardly the same Sir Matthew, in any sense, as the bullying growler who had driven by his side not two days ago. For *this* morning the double-seated buggy was the scene of neither plaints nor abuse. Quietly over the bush track—where last Monsieur Caloche, with hand to his breast, had run sobbing along—the two men drove, their wheels passing over a wideawake hat, lying neglected and dusty in the road. For more than an hour and a half they followed the track, the dusty soil that had been witness to the boy's flight still indicating at intervals traces of a small footprint. The oppressive calm of the atmosphere seemed to have left even the ridges of dust undisturbed. Blunt reflected that it must have been "rough on a fellow" to run all that way in the burning sun. It perplexed him, moreover, to remember that the shepherd's hut would be now far in their rear. Perhaps it was with a newly-born sense of uneasiness on his own account that he flicked his whip and made the trotter "go", for no comment could be expected from Sir Matthew, sitting in complete silence by his side.

To Blunt's discerning eyes the last of the footprints seemed to occur right in the middle of the track. On either side was the plain. Ostensibly, Sir Matthew had come that way to look at the sheep. There was, accordingly, every reason for turning to the right and driving towards a belt of timber some hundred yards away, and there were apparently more forcible reasons still for making for a particular tree—a straggling tree, with some pretensions to a meagre shade, the sight of which called forth an ejaculation, not entirely coherent, from Blunt.

Sir Matthew saw the cause of Blunt's ejaculation—a recumbent figure that had probably reached "the quiet haven of us all"—it lay so still. But whether quiet or no, it would seem that to disturb its peace was a matter of life or death to Sir Matthew Bogg. Yet surely here was satiety of the fullest for his hobby! Had he not "dropped on to the 'foreign adventurer' unawares?" So unawares, in fact, that Monsieur Caloche never heeded his presence, or the presence of his working manager, but lay with a glaze on his half-closed eyes in stiff unconcern at their feet.

The clerks and juniors in the outer office of the great firm of Bogg & Co. would have been at some loss to recognise their chief in the livid man who knelt by the dead lad's side. He wanted to feel his heart, it appeared, but his trembling fingers failed him. Blunt comprehended the gesture. Whatever of tenderness Monsieur Caloche had expended in his short lifetime was repaid by the gentleness with which the working manager passed his hand under the boy's rigid neck. It was with a shake of the head that seemed to Sir Matthew like the fiat of his doom that Blunt unbuttoned Monsieur Caloche's vest and discovered the fair, white throat beneath. Unbuttoning still—with tremulous fingers, and a strange apprehension creeping chillily over him—the manager saw the open vest fall loosely asunder, and then—

Yes; then it was proven that Sir Matthew's hobby had gone its extremest length. Though it could hardly have been rapture at its great triumph that filled his eyes with such a strange expression of horror as he stood looking fearfully down on the corpse at his feet. For he had, in point of fact, "dropped on to it unawares;" but it was no longer Monsieur Caloche he had "dropped on to," but a girl with breast of marble, bared in its cold whiteness to the open daylight, and to his ardent gaze. Bared, without any protest from the half-closed eyes, unconcerned behind the filmy veil which glazed them. A virgin breast, spotless in hue, save for a narrow purple streak, marking it in a dark line from the collar-bone downwards. Sir Matthew knew, and the working manager knew, and the child they called Monsieur Caloche had known, by whose hand the mark had been imprinted. It seemed to Sir Matthew that a similar mark, red hot like a brand, must now burn on his own forehead for ever.[26] For what if the hungry Australian sun, and emotion, and exhaustion had been the actual cause of the girl's death? he acknowledged, in the bitterness of his heart, that the "cause of the cause" was his own bloodstained hand.

It must have been poor satisfaction to his hobby, after this, to note that Blunt had found a tiny pocketbook on the person of the corpse, filled with minute foreign handwriting. Of which nothing could be made! For, with one exception, it was filled with French quotations, all of the same tenor—all pointing to the one conclusion—and clearly proving (if it has not been proved already) that a woman who loses her beauty loses her all. The English quotation will be known to some readers of Shakespeare, "So beauty

114

blemished once for ever's lost!" Affixed to it was the faintly-traced signature of Henriette Caloche.

So here was a sort of insight into the mystery. The "foreign adventurer" might be exonerated after all. No baser designs need be laid at the door of dead "Monsieur Caloche" than the design of hiding the loss which had deprived her of all glory in her sex. If, indeed, the loss were a *real* one! For beauty is more than skin-deep, although Monsieur Caloche had not known it. It is of the bone, and the fibre, and the nerves that thrill through the brain. It is of the form and the texture too, as any one would have allowed who scrutinised the body prone in the dust. Even the cruel scars seemed merciful now, and relaxed their hold on the chiselled features, as though "eloquent, just, and mightie Death" would suffer no hand but his own to dally with his possession.

It is only in Christmas stories, I am afraid, where, in deference to so rollicking a season, everything is bound to come right in the end, that people's natures are revolutionised in a night, and from narrow-minded villains they become open-hearted seraphs of charity. Still, it is on record of the first Henry that from the time of the sinking of the *White Ship* "he never smiled again." I cannot say that Sir Matthew was never known to smile, in his old sour way, or that he never growled or scolded, in his old bullying fashion, after the discovery of Monsieur Caloche's body. But he was none the less a changed man. The outside world might rightly conjecture that henceforth a slender, mournful-eyed shadow would walk by his side through life. But what can the outside world know of the refinement of mental anguish that may be endured by a mind awakened too late? In Sir Matthew's case— relatively as well as positively. For constant contemplation of a woman's pleading eyes and a dead statuesque form might give rise to imaginings that it would be maddening to dwell upon. What a wealth of caresses those stiff little hands had had it in their power to bestow! What a power of lighting up the solemnest office, and—be sure—the greatest, dreariest house, was latent in those dejected eyes?

Brooding is proverbially bad for the liver. Sir Matthew died of the liver complaint, and his will was cited as an instance of the eccentricity of a wealthy Australian, who, never having been in France, left the bulk of his money to the purpose of constructing and maintaining a magnificent wing to a smallpox hospital in the south of France. It was stipulated that it should be called the "Henriette" wing, and is, I believe, greatly admired by visitors from all parts of the world.

HIS MODERN GODIVA

The Lady Godiva, as every one will allow, is a hackneyed subject for a picture, but so, for that matter, is Joan of Arc or the Crucifixion. It requires all the genius of a Bastien-Lepage or a Bonnat; all the mystic realism of the one, all the well-nigh brutal power of the other—that *ouvrier en couleurs*,[27] as the French call him—to make the presentment of either the Maid or the Christ acceptable in a modern exhibition.

Edgar Freer was neither a Bastien-Lepage nor a Bonnat. Yet his "Lady Godiva" (*exposed*, as he called it, in the semi-French jargon of the English art-student in Paris, at the Salon of 188—) had just enough of the influence of both masters to arrest the attention of a jaded public of critics and sight-seers. For one thing, the picture was well hung, and for another, it was treated from a powerfully suggestive point of view. Its potential qualities were perhaps even more remarkable than its actual ones, for thereby hung a tale which was only known to two people in the world—to wit, the artist and his newly-married wife and model.

It was in the Luxembourg Gardens that Edgar Freer had first made her acquaintance. He was at work just then upon a picture of the heroine of *The Scarlet Letter*[28] to the order of a wealthy American Philistine of Puritan descent, and was seeking for a model with something more of a history in her eyes than the ordinary professional model could show. True, he could find in the Quartier Latin many grisettes of the type of the heroines in Murger's *Vie de Bohème*, with any amount of histories in their eyes. But it was the quality of the experience, not the quantity of it, that could alone impart the particular kind of expression he needed for his Hester Prynne; and it is to be feared, as regarded the grisettes, that their experiences were too frequent and free to leave upon their faces such a stamp as he could imagine the Puritan maid-mother might have worn.

Sitting one day upon a bench beneath one of the stiff, flat-chested effigies of the Queens of France, with the rays of the autumn sun filtering down through the yellowing chestnut leaves upon the *Petit Journal* on his knees, he saw his Hester for the first time walking across the gardens. It did not need more than a glance to tell him she had been accosted by the two young Frenchmen who were following her. Her head was up, her lips were set, there was a warm rose-colour in her cheeks, and her eyes had the defiant light that the stimulating consciousness of being given chase to for her outward attractions, and of resenting it, had imparted to them. Yielding to a sudden impulse, he rose and walked towards her, and, taking off his hat as she looked round in surprise, said in purest Oxford English:

"You are being annoyed, I can see. Pray let me see you through the gardens. You don't know Quartier Latin manners and customs."

"No, indeed I don't," she assented, the colour mounting still higher in her cheeks as she spoke; "and thank you; but I am not very far from where we are staying. It is only in the Rue Vavin."

This was the beginning of the friendship. Between the landmarks of the Queens of France and the Rue Vavin, Edgar managed to discover enough about his new acquaintance to carry away all her *dossier* in his mind. Name, Freda James; height, five feet four inches; age? not over twenty, surely, or thereabouts; personal appearance, delicious; profession, undetermined. Trying to do for herself. Not alone in the world, but one of nine too many at home. Present occupation, going about the Continent with vain and cross old lady, and hates it.

After two informal assignations, Edgar had secured his model. Upon her afternoons out, Freda became transformed in his studio into Hester Prynne, with the fantastically embroidered scarlet letter on her breast, and a baby lay-figure upon her arm. At first the artist allowed her to climb unaided the ninety odd steps that led to his artistically untidy *atelier* in the Rue Notre Dame des Champs; but after only two sittings he waited for her on the first, and then on the second landing. Every fresh flight of steps he descended marked a corresponding rise in his sentiment, until it came to his meeting her at the corner of the clattering Rue de Rennes itself. He would ransack the shops of the *pâtissiers* for the choicest *petits-fours*, and bribe her with these and afternoon tea to remain as Freda, after her pose as Hester was at an end.

The picturesque robe that the heroine of *The Scarlet Letter* is supposed to have worn upon the pillory having been but vaguely described by Hawthorne, Edgar allowed his fancy to run riot in the devising of it. One detail that he insisted upon was a finely embroidered kerchief crossed over the bust. As he adjusted it upon his model, he could not fail to admire her beautiful throat, marked off by the encircling line known as the *collier de Vénus*. At the end of the sitting he entreated Freda to allow him to do a rapid sketch of her as *une tête d'expression*, with bare neck and shoulders, and long brown gold hair descending upon the back. She demurred at first, but yielded finally, and in the gesture with which she performed the operation called in feminine language to unfasten a body, and bared her charming neck and arms to his gaze, he saw his opportunity for creating such an interpretation of Lady Godiva as had never yet been imagined.

He would have Freda array herself only in an old-world tunic or kirtle. Capital terms, those! he reflected—so elastic in their application, and quite reassuring; and what's in a name, after all? as Shakespeare says; and it should be just as she was on the point of yielding this her last intrench-ment, looking fearfully round, that he would paint his Lady Godiva. Her long coils of hair should be unbound, but not as yet shaken loose, and the picture should be replete with the delicate suggestion that seemed to him to be lacking in all the French presentments of the legend he had seen.

It still remained, however, to make Freda hear reason, which is also a phrase that may be variously interpreted. How it came about neither was exactly aware; but before the dress—or undress—rehearsals for the pose were at an end, Edgar's model had become his betrothed wife. And in the meantime the picture grew apace. In obedience to one of those over-mastering inspirations that come but once in a lifetime, he worked on at his canvas with feverish persistency. There seemed to be nothing to efface or correct. Just as Tennyson described the heroine of his poem

> *Looking like a summer moon*
> *Half dipped in cloud,*

so his Lady Godiva stood revealed against a synchronally harmonious background. More effective than whatsoever masterpiece of the fleshy school was the white perfection of arms and ankles; and perhaps the triumph of the achievement was the suggestion by which the kirtle appeared to have reached the very point of slipping from the polished shoulders to the ground. The *point de l'inconnu* added the crowning charm to the whole.

Yet both Edgar and his model were incapable of appreciating their joint work when the picture was forwarded for approval to the jury of the Salon. They heard that it was accepted, and in the interval that followed they went across the Channel to a London registry office and were married.

Upon their return to Paris, after a honeymoon ramble in Wales, Edgar found himself famous. His "Lady Godiva" was the *clou* of the Salon. He could hardly take up a daily paper in which he did not find some new and startling lie about himself. Piles of cards, photographs of would-be models, letters from artists and journalists, and—most astonishing of all—serious propositions from picture-dealers, lay in a heap in the *atelier* in which he and his wife intended to set up their Bohemian housekeeping.

Freda was wild with exultation; but after the first flush of triumph, Edgar became aware of the penalty he must pay for his success. His picture was famous, *and so was his wife.* It was nothing but her living portrait that was gathering from day to day, and from hour to hour, the eager crowd; and not only the crowd of connoisseurs and critics, but the crowd for whom the picture was nothing and the model everything.

The first time he went to the Salon with Freda on his arm they were literally mobbed. The likeness was too startling not to be recognised at once, and all manner of eyes that had been wandering over "Lady Godiva's" arms and ankles seemed now to be converted into drills, that sought to pierce through the little Bon Marché mantilla that the artist's wife wore over her shoulders, and the clocked stockings she had added after much hesitation to her scanty trousseau for extra occasions.

Her fashion of standing fire was to assume unconsciously the self-same expression that had so captivated Edgar the first time he had seen her. He had compared it then in his own mind to that of some nymph of antiquity about to metamorphosize herself into a stream or a flower to disconcert the pursuit of a too persistent admirer. But now he began to doubt whether, in the place of such a nymph, Freda would have consented to be metamorphosized at all.

The doubt became a torment to him. Besides the artistic temperament he had the misfortune to possess the particular kind of unreasoning jealousy defined in certain dictionaries as the quality of being suspiciously fearful. Under this influence all his triumph in the success of his picture was merged into bitter remorse at having painted it. What was it, after all, but an advertisement of the charms of his wife? and what assurance had he that this result was as distasteful— nay, as odious—to her as to himself? For the matter of that, how could he be certain that it was distasteful to her at all? Why, if it were otherwise, did she allow him to leave the picture in the Salon, and suffer his "Lady Godiva" to be brought down to the level of the latest professional beauty?

While he was a prey to these and similar torments inflicted by the green-eyed monster, Edgar received a letter from a princely patron of art who had also the reputation of being one of those who "come, and see, and conquer" as easily as the great Caesar himself, though in a different direction.

It was a letter that expressed the highest admiration of "Lady Godiva", and held out more than a hope of the ultimate purchase of the picture. The writer, moreover, begged permission to make Mr. Freer's personal acquaintance, and to be allowed the honour of visiting his studio at a specified hour the day after the Salon should be closed.

Edgar's perplexity upon the receipt of this missive was great. Had it been prophesied to him only a few weeks ago that Fame and Fortune would shortly knock at his door, and that he would hesitate about admitting them, he would have said that the prophecy lied. Yet here he was actually debating with himself whether he would receive the princely patron or his offer at all. After long reflection, with his forehead buried in his hands, he looked up suddenly from the open letter before him to his wife. She was moving lightly about his studio, filling his old china with the heavy-budded pink peonies that would blossom ere long into masses of silky rose-coloured petals. It seemed to him as though she had undergone something of a similar transformation since he had first seen her, disclosing undivined graces and allurements every day. But what if she were really a coquette at heart? What if she should have a fancy for resuming the *rôle* of the nymph escaping from her pursuers? The thought brought an unendurable sting in its wake; yet how, he asked himself, could he escape from this nightmare of his own creation?

The same day he had an inspiration. It was while his wife was posing for the still unfinished picture of Hester Prynne. To beguile the time, he would tell her upon these occasions tales of his student life in Paris, and make her recount her life as one of the nine too many at home. This afternoon he chose a different theme. He wandered back to early English history, and recalled to Freda the episode of the Saxon lord who begged his wife, the beautiful Elfrida, to disguise herself in a hideous garb when Ethelred the King came to visit them.

"For they both knew, don't you know," he added, "that it was really only to see *her* that the King took it into his head to come at all. I wonder what *you* would say, Freda, if I were to ask you to do the same thing? Just suppose, now, I were to say, 'My dear child, Lord So-and-so—the Duc de Monplaisir, for instance—is coming the day after to-morrow, and I want you to make a real "sight" of yourself for my sake. You must get up a thirty-inch waist, and put on the most unbecoming bonnet you can find, and you must have a thick veil, with just an artistically deformed nose shadowed out behind it,' what would you say?"

"What's the use of being so silly?" objected Freda. "In the first place, the Duc de Monplaisir isn't coming—"

"But he is. He's coming to buy our picture."

"To buy our picture! Not really? O Edgar, I can hardly believe it! There's no mistake about your being *arrivé* now."

Her eyes shone, her face beamed with pleasure. "And he's coming here! To this very place? Coming to our *atelier?*" she insisted.

Edgar's face darkened. "Now for the test," he thought grimly; and in words of passionate entreaty he conjured his wife to grant him this first and only proof of her affection he would ask of her.

"You may say I am mad," he pleaded. "I have no right to ask such a favour of you, I know; it is unreasonable and monstrous. But I love you, Freda, and—and—there are things you can't understand. I have staked what is far more than my life to me on your making this sacrifice."

It was in vain that his wife sought to argue the question objectively. Edgar admitted that she had all the reason on her side. It was the very unreasonableness of his request, coupled with his own intense feeling about it, that rendered it so crucial a test. "Love counteth not the cost," he thought. "If she has a spark of real love for me, she will yield."

But Freda would be bound by no promises, and as the eventful morning drew near, Edgar's agitation increased to fever-height. The famous picture had been sent for to the Salon the previous day, and now stood in the most favourable light against the wall of the *atelier*. "Lady Godiva" looked more alluring than ever in her unsupported beauty, and "Lady Godiva's" author stood pale and haggard in front of his work, waiting for the promised purchaser like a criminal awaiting condemnation.

A knock, and the Duc de Monplaisir, with an eyeglass in his left eye and a cane in his hand, the perfect present-ment of a *boulevardier de la haute gamme*, entered. Though his glance round the studio occupied an almost imperceptible flash of time, it was sufficient to confirm Edgar in his preconceived impression that the purchase of the picture was the ostensible and not the real motive of the visit. His heart beat furiously as his visitor addressed him a few well-chosen compliments on his work. He hardly understood or even heard what was said to him. He was waiting for Freda to enter.

The handle turned at last. A portly woman of the *bourgeoise* type, with her face bound round like that of a victim to chronic toothache, behind a heavy black veil that only half concealed a carnival nose, came tramping into the room. But if the vision had been that of an angel of light, it could not have brought more radiance into the artist's face. The Duke's face, on the other hand, grew proportionately long. He bowed doubtfully, and turned away. If he had hesitated about taking the picture before, it was now evident that he was anxious to cry off altogether. At this critical moment there was a slight exclamation from the artist's wife, which made him start and look round. Her cloak had apparently caught in a nail, and, as though by magic, cloak, bonnet, veil, and carnival nose had fallen to the ground in a heap, and the original Lady Godiva, in clinging morning-gown, with all her beauty heightened and intensified by the excitement of the moment, stood revealed as Mrs. Edgar Freer.

Hardly conscious of what was passing, Edgar saw the swift and unmistakable change in his visitor's manner. He commanded himself sufficiently to feign acceptance of the splendid offer made him, and found a pretext for hurrying the purchaser away. When he returned to the *atelier*, Freda was picking up her disguise with a brilliant flush of triumph on her cheeks.

"You foolish old fellow!" she said. "You nearly spoiled all our chances of selling the picture. If I had not come to the rescue just in time!"

"If you had not come to the rescue," he repeated, with a smile that seemed somehow to make his wife's heart stand still, "if you had not come to the rescue—this, and this, and this would never have happened."

And before her horrified eyes he took up a knife that was lying on the table, and cut and stabbed his beautiful "Lady Godiva", face and neck and arms and ankles, through and through. The masterpiece was destroyed, and the spirit that inspired it could never again descend upon its author.

AN OLD-TIME EPISODE IN TASMANIA

The gig was waiting upon the narrow gravel drive in front of the fuchsia-wreathed porch of Cowa Cottage. Perched upon the seat, holding the whip in two small, plump, ungloved hands, sat Trucaninny, Mr. Paton's youngest daughter, whose straw-coloured, sun-steeped hair, and clear, sky-reflecting eyes, seemed to protest against the name of a black gin that some "clay-brained cleric" had bestowed upon her irresponsible little person at the baptismal font some eight or nine years ago. The scene of this outrage was Old St. David's Cathedral, Hobart,—or, as it was then called, Hobart *Town*,—chief city of the Arcadian island of Tasmania; and just at this moment, eight o'clock on a November morning, the said cathedral tower, round and ungainly, coated with a surface of dingy white plaster, reflected back the purest, brightest light in the world. From Trucaninny's perch—she had taken the driver's seat—she could see, not only the cathedral, but a considerable portion of the town, which took the form of a capital S as it followed the windings of the coast. Beyond the wharves, against which a few whalers and fishing-boats were lying idle, the middle distance was represented by the broad waters of the Derwent, radiantly blue, and glittering with silver sparkles; while the far-off background showed a long stretch of yellow sand, and the hazy, undulating outline of low-lying purple hills. Behind her the aspect was different. Tiers of hills rose one above the other in grand confusion, until they culminated in the towering height of Mount Wellington, keeping guard in majestic silence over the lonely little city that encircled its base. This portion of the view, however, was hidden from Trucaninny's gaze by the weatherboard cottage in front of which the gig was standing,— though I doubt whether in any case she would have turned

127

her head to look at it; the faculty of enjoying a beautiful landscape being an acquisition of later years than she had attained since the perpetration of the afore-mentioned outrage of her christening. Conversely, as Herbert Spencer says, the young man who was holding the horse's head until such time as the owner of the gig should emerge from the fuchsia-wreathed porch, fastened his eyes upon the beautiful scene before him with more than an artist's appreciation in their gaze. He was dressed in the rough clothes of a working gardener, and so much of his head as could be seen beneath the old felt wide-awake that covered it, bore ominous evidence of having been recently shaved. I use the word ominous advisedly, for a shaven head in connection with a working suit had nothing priestly in its suggestion, and could bear, indeed, only one interpretation in the wicked old times in Tasmania. The young man keeping watch over the gig had clearly come into that fair scene for his country's good; and the explanation of the absence of a prison suit was doubtless due to the fact he was out on a ticket-of-leave. What the landscape had to say to him under these circumstances was not precisely clear. Perhaps all his soul was going out towards the white-sailed wool-ship tacking down the Bay on the first stage of a journey of most uncertain length; or possibly the wondrous beauty of the scene, contrasted with the unspeakable horror of the one he had left, brought the vague impression that it was merely some exquisite vision. That a place so appalling as his old prison should exist in the heart of all this peace and loveliness, seemed too strange an anomaly. Either that was a nightmare and this was real, or this was a fantastic dream and that was the revolting truth; but then which was which, and how had he, Richard Cole, late No. 213, come to be mixed up with either?

As though to give a practical answer to his melancholy question, the sharp tingle of a whip's lash made itself felt at this instant across his cheek. In aiming the cumbersome driving-whip at the persistent flies exploring the mare's back, Trucaninny had brought it down in a direction she had not intended it to take. For a moment she stood aghast. Richard's face was white with passion. He turned fiercely round; his flaming eyes seemed literally to send out sparks of anger. "Oh, please, I didn't mean it," cried the child penitently. "I wanted to hit the flies. I did indeed. I hope I didn't hurt you?"

The *amende honorable* brought about an immediate reaction. The change in the young man's face was wonderful to behold. As he smiled back full reassurance at the offender, it might be seen that his eyes could express the extremes of contrary feeling at the very shortest notice. For all answer, he raised his old felt wide-awake in a half-mocking though entirely courtly fashion, like some nineteenth century Don César de Bazan, and made a graceful bow.

"Are *you* talking to the man, Truca?" cried a querulous voice at this moment from the porch, with a stress on the you that made the little girl lower her head, shame-faced. "What do you mean by disobeying orders, miss?"

The lady who swept out upon the verandah at the close of this tirade was in entire accord with her voice. "British matron" would have been the complete description of Miss Paton, if fate had not willed that she should be only a British spinster. The inflexibility that comes of finality of opinion regarding what is proper and what is the reverse,—a rule of conduct that is of universal application for the true British matron,—expressed itself in every line of her face and in every fold of her gown. That she was relentlessly respectable and unyielding might be read at the first glance; that she had been handsome, in the same hard way, a great many years before Truca was maltreated at the baptismal font, might also have been guessed at from present indications. But that she should be the "own sister" of the good-looking, military-moustached, debonair man (I use the word debonair here in the French sense) who now followed her out of the porch, was less easy to divine. The character of the features as well as of the expression spoke of two widely differing temperaments. Indeed, save for a curious dent between the eyebrows, and a something in the nostrils that seemed to say he was not to be trifled with, Mr. Paton might have sat for the portrait of one of those jolly good fellows who reiterate so tunefully that they "won't go home till morning", and who are as good as their word afterwards.

Yet "jolly good fellow" as he showed himself in card-rooms and among so-called boon companions, he could reveal himself in a very different light to the convicts who fell under his rule. Forming part of a system for the crushing down of the unhappy prisoners, in accordance with the principle of "Woe be to him through whom the offence cometh," he could return with a light heart to his breakfast or his dinner, after seeing some score of his fellow-men abjectly writhing under the lash, or pinioned in a ghastly row upon the hideous gallows. "Use," says Shakespeare, "can almost change the stamp of Nature." In Mr. Paton's case it had warped as well as changed it. Like the people who live in the atmosphere of Courts, and come to regard all outsiders as another and inferior race, he had come to look upon humanity as divisible into two classes—namely, those who were convicts, and those who were not. For the latter, he had still some ready drops of the milk of human kindness at his disposal. For the former, he had no more feeling than we have for snakes or sharks, as the typical and popular embodiments of evil.

Miss Paton had speedily adopted her brother's views in this respect. Summoned from England to keep house for him at the death of Trucaninny's mother, she showed an aptitude for introducing prison discipline into her domestic rule. From constant association with the severe *régime* that she was accustomed to see exercised upon the convicts, she had ended by regarding disobedience to orders, whether in children or in servants, as the unpardonable sin. One of her laws, as of the Medes and Persians, was that the young people in the Paton household should never exchange a word with the convict servants in their father's employ. It was hard to observe the letter of the law in the case of the indoor

servants, above all for Truca, who was by nature a garrulous
little girl. Being a truthful little girl as well, she was often
obliged to confess to having had a talk with the latest
importation from the gaol,—an avowal which signified, as
she well knew, the immediate forfeiture of all her week's
pocket-money.

On the present occasion her apologies to the gardener were
the latest infringement of the rule. She looked timidly towards
her aunt as the latter advanced austerely in the direction
of the gig, but, to her relief, Miss Paton hardly seemed to
notice her.

"I suppose you will bring the creature back with you,
Wilfrid?" she said, half-questioningly, half-authoritatively,
as her brother mounted into the gig and took the reins from
Truca's chubby hands. "Last time we had a drunkard *and*
a thief. The time before, a thief, and—and a—really I don't
know which was worse. It is frightful to be reduced to such
a choice of evils, but I would almost suggest your looking
among the—you know—the—*in-fan-ti-cide* cases this time."

She mouthed the word in separate syllables at her brother,
fearful of pronouncing it openly before Truca and the convict
gardener.

Mr. Paton nodded. It was not the first time he had been
sent upon the delicate mission of choosing a maid for his
sister from the female prison, politely called the Factory,
at the foot of Mount Wellington. For some reason it would
be difficult to explain, his selections were generally rather
more successful than hers. Besides which, it was a satisfaction
to have some one upon whom to throw the responsibility
of the inevitable catastrophe that terminated the career of
every successive ticket-of-leave in turn.

The morning, as we have seen, was beautiful. The gig
bowled smoothly over the macadamized length of Macquarie
Street. Truca was allowed to drive; and so deftly did her
little fingers guide the mare, that her father lighted his cigar,
and allowed himself to ruminate upon a thousand things
that it would have been better perhaps to leave alone. In

certain moods he was apt to deplore the fate that had landed—
or stranded—him in this God-forsaken corner of the world.
Talk of prisoners, indeed! What was he himself but a prisoner,
since the day when he had madly passed sentence of
transportation on himself and his family, because the pay
of a Government clerk in England did not increase in the
same ratio as the income-tax. As a matter of fact, he did
not wear a canary-coloured livery, and his prison was as
near an approach, people said, to an earthly Paradise as could
well be conceived. With its encircling chains of mountains,
folded one around the other, it was like a mighty rose, tossed
from the Creator's hand into the desolate Southern Ocean.
Here to his right towered purple Mount Wellington, with
rugged cliffs gleaming forth from a purple background. To
his left the wide Derwent shone and sparkled in blue robe
and silver spangles, like the Bay of Naples, he had been
told. Well, he had never seen the Bay of Naples, but there
were times when he would have given all the beauty here,
and as much more to spare, for a strip of London pavement in front of his old club. Mr. Paton's world, indeed,
was out of joint. Perhaps twelve years of unthinking
acquiescence in the flogging and hanging of convicts had
distorted his mental focus. As for the joys of home-life, he
told himself that those which had fallen to his share brought
him but cold comfort. His sister was a Puritan, and she
was making his children hypocrites, with the exception,
perhaps, of Truca. Another disagreeable subject of reflection
was the one that his groom Richard was about to leave
him. In a month's time, Richard, like his royal namesake,
would be himself again. For the past five years he had been
only No. 213, expiating in that capacity a righteous blow
aimed at a cowardly ruffian who had sworn to marry his
sister—by fair means or by foul. The blow had been only
too well aimed. Richard was convicted of manslaughter, and
sentenced to seven years' transportation beyond the seas. His
sister, who had sought to screen him, was tried and condemned
for perjury. Of the latter, nothing was known. Of the former,

Mr. Paton only knew that he would be extremely loth to part with so good a servant. Silent as the Slave of the Lamp, exact as any machine, performing the least of his duties with the same intelligent scrupulousness, his very presence in the household was a safeguard and a reassurance. It was like his luck, Mr. Paton reflected in his present pessimistic mood, to have chanced upon such a fellow, just as by his d——d good conduct he had managed to obtain a curtailment of his sentence. If Richard had been justly dealt with, he would have had two good years left to devote to the service of his employer. As to keeping him after he was a free man, that was not to be hoped for. Besides which, Mr. Paton was not sure that he should feel at all at his ease in dealing with a free man. The slave-making instinct, which is always inherent in the human race, whatever civilisation may have done to repress it, had become his sole rule of conduct in his relations with those who served him.

There was one means perhaps of keeping the young man in bondage, but it was a means that even Mr. Paton himself hesitated to employ. By an almost superhuman adherence to impossible rules, Richard had escaped hitherto the humiliation of the lash; but if a flogging could be laid to his charge, his time of probation would be of necessity prolonged, and he might continue to groom the mare and tend the garden for an indefinite space of time, with the ever intelligent thoroughness that distinguished him. A slip of paper in a sealed envelope, which the victim would carry himself to the nearest justice of the peace, would effect the desired object. The etiquette of the proceeding did not require that any explanation should be given.

Richard would be fastened to the triangles, and any subsequent revolt on his part could only involve him more deeply than before. Mr. Paton had no wish to hurt him; but he was after all an invaluable servant, and perhaps he would be intelligent enough to understand that the disagreeable formality to which he was subjected was in reality only a striking mark of his master's esteem for him.

133

Truca's father had arrived thus far in his meditations when the gig pulled up before the Factory gate. It was a large bare building, with white unshaded walls, but the landscape which framed it gave it a magnificent setting. The little girl was allowed to accompany her father indoors, while a man in a grey prison suit, under the immediate surveillance of an armed warder, stood at the mare's head.

Mr. Paton's mission was a delicate one. To gently scan his brother man, and still gentler sister woman, did not apply to his treatment of convicts. He brought his sternest official expression to bear upon the aspirants who defiled past him at the matron's bidding, in their disfiguring prison livery. One or two, who thought they detected a likely looking man behind the Government official, threw him equivocal glances as they went by. Of these he took no notice. His choice seemed to lie in the end between a sullen-looking elderly woman, whom the superintendent qualified as a "sour jade", and a half-imbecile girl, when his attention was suddenly attracted to a new arrival, who stood out in such marked contrast with the rest that she looked like a dove in the midst of a flock of vultures.

"Who is that?" he asked the matron in a peremptory aside.

"That, sir,"—the woman's lips assumed a tight expression as she spoke,—"she's No. 27—Amelia Clare—she came out with the last batch."

"Call her up, will you?" was the short rejoinder, and the matron reluctantly obeyed.

In his early days Truca's father had been a great lover of Italian opera. There was hardly an air of Bellini's or Donizetti's that he did not know by heart. As No. 27 came slowly towards him, something in her manner of walking, coupled with the half-abstracted, half-fixed expression in her beautiful grey eyes, reminded him of Amina in the *Sonnambula*.[27] So strong, indeed, was the impression, that he would hardly have been surprised to see No. 27 take off her unbecoming prison cap and jacket, and disclose two round white arms to match her face, or to hear her sing "*Ah! non giunge*" in soft dreamy tones. He could have hummed or whistled a tuneful second himself at a moment's notice, for the matter of that. However, save in the market scene in *Martha*, there is no precedent for warbling a duet with the young person you are about to engage as a domestic servant. Mr. Paton remembered this in time, and confined himself to what the French call *le strict nécessaire*. He inquired of Amelia whether she could do fine sewing, and whether she could clear-starch. His sister had impressed these questions upon him, and he was pleased with himself for remembering them.

Amelia, or Amina (she was really very like Amina), did not reply at once. She had to bring her mind back from the far-away sphere to which it had wandered, or, in other words, to pull herself together first. When the reply did come, it was uttered in just the low, melodious tones one might have expected. She expressed her willingness to attempt whatever was required of her, but seemed very diffident as regarded her power of execution. "I have forgotten so many things," she concluded, with a profound sigh.

"*Sir*, you impertinent minx," corrected the matron.

Amelia did not seem to hear, and her new employer hastened to interpose.

"We will give you a trial," he said, in a curiously modified tone, "and I hope you won't give me any occasion to regret it."

The necessary formalities were hurried through. Mr. Paton disregarded the deferential disclaimers of the matron, but experienced, nevertheless, something of a shock when he saw Amelia divested of her prison garb. She had a thorough-bred air that discomfited him. Worse still, she was undeniably pretty. The scissors that had clipped her fair locks had left a number of short rings that clung like tendrils round her shapely little head. She wore a black stuff jacket of extreme simplicity and faultless cut, and a little black bonnet that might have been worn by a Nursing Sister or a "*grande dame*" with equal appropriateness. Thus attired, her appearance was so effective, that Mr. Paton asked himself whether he was not doing an unpardonably rash thing in driving No. 27 down Macquarie Street in his gig, and introducing her into his household afterwards.

It was not Truca, for she had "driven and lived" that morning, whose *mauvais quart-d'heure* was now to come. It was her father's turn to fall under its influence, as he sat, stern and rigid, on the driver's seat, with his little girl nestling up to him as close as she was able, and that strange, fair, mysterious presence on the other side, towards which he had the annoyance of seeing all the heads of the passers-by turn as he drove on towards home.

Arrived at Cowa Cottage, the young gardener ran forward to open the gate; and here an unexpected incident occurred. As Richard's eyes rested upon the new arrival, he uttered an exclamation that caused her to look round. Their eyes met, a flash of instant recognition was visible in both. Then, like the night that follows a sudden discharge of electricity, the gloom that was habitual to both faces settled down upon them once more. Richard shut the gate with his accustomed machine-like precision. Amelia looked at the intangible something in the clouds that had power to fix her gaze upon itself. Yet the emotion she had betrayed was not lost upon her employer. Who could say? As No. 213 and No. 27, these two might have crossed each other's paths before. That the convicts had wonderful and incomprehensible means of communicating with each other, was well known to Mr. Paton. That young men and young women have an equal facility for understanding each other, was also a fact he did not ignore. But which of these two explanations might account for the signs of mutual recognition and sympathy he had just witnessed? Curiously enough, he felt, as he pondered over the mystery later in the day, that he should prefer the former solution. An offensive and defensive alliance was well known to exist among the convicts, and he told himself that he could meet and deal with the difficulties arising from such a cause as he had met and dealt with them before. That was a matter which came within his province, but the taking into account of any sentimental kind of rubbish did *not* come within his province. For some unaccountable reason, the thought of having Richard flogged presented itself anew at this junction to his mind. He put it away, as he had done before, angered with himself for having harboured it. But it returned at intervals during the succeeding week, and was never stronger than one afternoon, when his little girl ran out to him as he sat smoking in the verandah, with an illustrated volume of *Grimm's Tales* in her hands.

"Oh, papa, look! I've found some one just like Amelia in my book of Grimm. It's the picture of Snow-White. Only look, papa! Isn't it the very living image of Amelia?"

"Nonsense!" said her father; but he looked at the page nevertheless. Truca was right. The snow-maiden in the woodcut had the very eyes and mouth of Amelia Clare— frozen through some mysterious influence into beautiful, unyielding rigidity. Mr. Paton wished sometimes he had never brought the girl into his house. Not that there was any kind of fault to be found with her. Even his sister, who might have passed for "She-who-must-be-obeyed," if Rider Haggard's books had existed at that time, could not complain of want of docile obedience to orders on the part of the new maid. Nevertheless, her presence was oppressive to the master of the house. Two lines of Byron's haunted him constantly in connection with her—

> *So coldly sweet, so deadly fair,*
> *We start—for life is wanting there.*

If Richard worked like an automaton, then she worked like a spirit; and when she moved noiselessly about the room where he happened to be sitting, he could not help following her uneasily with his eyes.

The days wore on, succeeding each other and resembling each other, as the French proverb has it, with desperate monotony. Christmas, replete with roses and strawberries, had come and gone. Mr. Paton was alternately swayed by two demons, one of which whispered in his ear, "Richard Cole is in love with No. 27. The time for him to regain his freedom is at hand. The first use he will make of it will be to leave you, and the next to marry Amelia Clare. You will thus be deprived of everything at one blow. You will lose the best man-servant you have ever known, and your sister, the best maid. And more than this, you will lose an interest in life that gives it a stimulating flavour it has not had for many a long year. Whatever may be the impulse that prompts you to wonder what that ice-bound face and form hide, it is an impulse that makes your heart beat and your blood course warmly through your veins. When this fair, uncanny presence is removed from your home, your life will become stagnant as it was before." To this demon Mr. Paton would reply energetically, "I won't give the fellow the chance of marrying No. 27. As soon as he has his freedom, I will give him the sack, and forbid him the premises. As for Amelia, she is my prisoner, and I would send her back to gaol to-morrow if I thought there were any nonsense up between her and him."

At this point demon No. 2 would intervene: "There is a better way of arranging matters. You have it in your power to degrade the fellow in his own eyes and in those of the girl he is after. There is more covert insolence in that impenetrable exterior of his than you have yet found out. Only give him proper provocation, and you will have ample justification for bringing him down. A good flogging would put everything upon its proper footing,—you would keep your servant and you would put a stop to the nonsense that is very probably going on. But don't lose too much time; for if you wait until the last moment, you will betray your hand. The fellow is useful to him, they will say of Richard, but it is rather rough upon him to be made aware of it in such a way as that."

One evening in January, Mr. Paton was supposed to be

at his club. In reality he was seated upon a bench in a bushy part of the garden, known as the shrubbery—in parley with the demons. The night had come down upon him almost without his being aware of it—a night heavy with heat and blackness, and noisy with the cracking and whirring of the locusts entombed in the dry soil. All at once he heard a slight rustling in the branches behind him. There was a light pressure of hands on his shoulders, and a face that felt like velvet to the touch was laid against his cheeks. Two firm, warm feminine lips pressed themselves upon his, and a voice that he recognised as Amelia's said in caressing tones, "Dearest Dick, have I kept you waiting?"

Had it been proposed to our hero some time ago that he should change places with No. 213, he would have declared that he would rather die first. But at this instant the convict's identity seemed so preferable to his own, that he hardly ventured to breathe lest he should betray the fact that he was only his own forlorn self. His silence disconcerted the intruder.

"Why don't you answer, Dick?" she asked impatiently.

"Answer? What am I to say?" responded her master. "I am not in the secret."

Amelia did not give him time to say more. With a cry of terror she turned and fled, disappearing as swiftly and mysteriously as she had come. The words "Dearest Dick" continued to ring in Mr. Paton's ears long after she had gone; and the more persistently the refrain was repeated, the more he felt tempted to give Richard a taste of his quality. He had tried to provoke him to some act of overt insolence in vain. He had worried and harried and insulted him all he could. The convict's constancy had never once deserted him. That his employer should have no pretext whereby he might have him degraded and imprisoned, he had acted upon the scriptural precept of turning his left cheek when he was smitten on the right. There were times when his master felt something of a persecutor's impotent rage against him. But now at least he felt he had entire justification for making an example of him. He would teach the fellow to play Romeo and Juliet with a fellow-convict behind his back. So thoroughly did the demon indoctrinate Mr. Paton with these ideas, that he felt next morning as though he were doing the most righteous action in the world, when he called Richard to him after breakfast, and said in a tone which he tried to render as careless as of custom, "Here, you! Just take this note over to Mr. Merton with my compliments, and *wait for the answer.*"

There was nothing in this command to cause the person who received it to grow suddenly livid. Richard had received such an order at least a score of times before, and had carried messages to and fro between his master and the justice of the peace with no more emotion than the occasion was worth. But on this particular morning, as he took the fatal note into his hands, he turned deadly pale. Instead of retreating with it in his customary automatic fashion, he fixed his eyes upon his employer's face, and something in their expression actually constrained Mr. Paton to lower his own.

"May I speak a word with you, sir?" he said, in low, uncertain tones.

It was the first time such a thing had happened, and it seemed to Richard's master that the best way of meeting it would be to "damn" the man and send him about his business.

But Richard did not go. He stood for an instant with his head thrown back, and the desperate look of an animal at bay in his eyes. At this critical moment a woman's form suddenly interposed itself between Mr. Paton and his victim. Amelia was there, looking like Amina after she had awoken from her trance. She came close to her master,—she had never addressed him before,—and raised her liquid eyes to his.

"You will not be hard on—my brother, sir, for the mistake I made last night?"

"Who said I was going to be hard on him?" retorted Mr. Paton, too much taken aback to find any more dignified form of rejoinder. "And if he is your brother, why do you wait until it is dark to indulge in your family effusions?"

The question was accompanied by a through and through look, before which Amelia did not quail.

"Have I your permission to speak to him in the day-time, sir?" she said submissively.

"I will institute an inquiry," interrupted her master. "Here, go about your business," he added, turning to Richard; "fetch out the mare, and hand me back that note. I'll ride over with it myself."

Three weeks later Richard Cole was a free man, and within four months from the date upon which Mr. Paton had driven Amelia Clare down Macquarie Street in his gig, she came to take respectful leave of him, dressed in the identical close-fitting jacket and demure little bonnet he remembered. Thenceforth she was nobody's bondswoman. He had a small heap of coin in readiness to hand over to her, with the payment of which, and a few gratuitous words of counsel on his part, the leave-taking would have been definitely and decorously accomplished. To tell her that he was more loth than ever to part with her, did not enter into the official programme. She was her own mistress now, as much or more so than the Queen of England herself, and it was hardly to be wondered at if the first use she made of her freedom was to shake the dust of Cowa Cottage off her feet. Still, if she had only known—if she had only known. It seemed too hard to let her go with the certainty that she never did or could know. Was it not for her sake that he had been swayed by all the conflicting impulses that had made him a changed man of late? For her that he had so narrowly escaped being a criminal awhile ago, and for her that he was appearing in the novel *rôle* of a reformer of the convict system now? He never doubted that she would have under-stood him if she *had* known. But to explain was out of the question. He must avow either all or nothing, and the all meant more than he dared to admit even to himself.

This was the reason why Amelia Clare departed sphinxlike as she had come. A fortnight after she had gone, as Mr. Paton was gloomily smoking by his library fire in the early dark of a wintry August evening, a letter bearing the N. S. Wales postmark was handed to him. The handwriting, very small and fine, had something familiar in its aspect. He broke open the seal,—letters were still habitually sealed in those days,—and read as follows:—

"SIR,—I am prompted to make you a confession—why, I cannot say, for I shall probably never cross your path again. I was married last week to Richard Cole, who was not my brother, as I led you to suppose, but my affianced husband, in whose behalf I would willingly suffer again to be unjustly condemned and transported. I have the warrant of Scripture for having assumed, like Sarah, the *rôle* of sister in preference to that of wife; besides which, it is hard to divest myself of an instinctive belief that the deceit was useful to Richard on one occasion. I trust you will pardon me.—Yours respectfully,

"AMELIA COLE."

The kindly phase Mr. Paton had passed through with regard to his convict victims came to an abrupt termination. The reaction was terrible. His name is inscribed among those "who foremost shall be damn'd to Fame" in Tasmania.

NOTES

1 Bill Sykes is a villain and henchman of Fagin in Charles Dickens' *Oliver Twist*. Next the desirable monster will be linked with Count Francesco Cenci, the bloody and incestuous tyrant-figure from Shelley's *The Cenci*.

2 Victor Frankenstein is the ill-advised creator in Mary Shelley's *Frankenstein*, whose scientific and inventive gifts culminate in a hideous monster.

3 Sir Joshua Reynolds was the dominant painter in eighteenth-century Britain. He was President of the Royal Academy as well as the leading portrait painter of the age, and did much to elevate the status of the artist in England.

4 John ("Jack") Ketch was an English hangman who died in 1686, and whose name became identified with the executioner figure in Punch and Judy puppet shows in England.

5 Hebe was a Greek goddess identified with perennial youth, and a cupbearer of the gods. She was also thought to be able to restore gods and men to their original vigour.

6 Hamadryads, in classical literature, were nymphs who lived in the country and were the tutelary spirits of trees, with which they were said to live and die.

7 The mortal woman, Psyche, enjoyed the embraces of the god Cupid at night, and was warned against seeking to fathom his identity. Jealous tongues, however, aroused her curiosity and fear. Breaking her oath she tried to see him with the aid of a lamp, and so lost her lover. Mrs Jason's "lover/husband", of course, is no Cupid, nor is there any easy way for her to gain release from her bond.

8 Solon was a sage lawgiver of antiquity. His response to the fabulously wealthy king of Lydia, Croesus, was "Call no man happy until he is dead". For good measure he added that Croesus was not the happiest of mortals, but a more humble Athenian who had pursued domestic and public virtue, and had fallen in the service of his state. Croesus was later defeated by the Persian king Cyrus, who condemned him to be burnt alive.

As the sentence was being carried out, Croesus called out
Solon's name in a manner which moved Cyrus, and earnt him
a reprieve.

9 In La Fontaine's fable, the ant or "fourmi" works throughout
the fine summer weather to ensure herself of plenty in winter;
whereas the grasshopper, despite warnings, idles his time
away, and eventually suffers accordingly.

10 Abishag was a beautiful virgin, chosen as a member of the
household of David to comfort him in his old age
(1 Kings, i, 1–4).

11 Chiron, half-man and half-horse, excelled his peers in his
mastery of music, medicine and archery. This renown made
him the chosen teacher of many of Greece's greatest heroes,
including Achilles, Hercules and Jason.

12 Amphion, a famous poet and musician, is said to have moved
stones and raised the walls of Thebes at the sound of his lyre.

13 Pactolus was the famous river in Lydia where Midas turned
into gold all he touched, including its sands.

14 *minauderies* is a French expression denoting affected and
flirtatious manners, coquettish ways.

15 Laurence Sterne was ranked amongst the foremost authors of
the sentimental novel for such works as *A Sentimental Journey
through France and Italy*, where characters are frequently
moved to excessive tears.

16 Andromeda, according to legend, was offered up as a victim to
appease the wrath of the gods. She was tied naked to a rock as
the intended prey for a sea-monster, but was rescued and
subsequently married by Perseus.

17 In Thackeray's *Vanity Fair*, Dobbin's love for Amelia remains
unchanged after she marries the vainglorious George Osborne,
and even later when, as a widow, she elevates her deceased
husband into an unlikely exemplar of masculine perfection.

18 In 1871 Napoleon III lost the Franco-Prussian war and with it
the French crown. The Third Republic was then established in
France, but was long rendered insecure by the plots of various
political groups, including those who sought to restore the
Bonaparte family to power.

19 Briareus was a warlike giant with one hundred hands and fifty heads.

20 A Barmecides' Feast is one where the dishes are empty and everything imaginary: it tantalises rather than allays hunger. The Barmecides were a great Persian family, famous for their wealth and power.

21 Pangloss was the incorrigibly optimistic philosopher and tutor of Voltaire's *Candide*, who preached that "all is for the best in this the best of all possible worlds".

22 Peri in Persian mythology were originally associated with an evil genius, or beautiful but malevolent sprite, but were later also linked with good presiding spirits.

23 An entozoon is a parasitic animal which lives within another.

24 The French government eventually yielded Paris to the triumphant combined German forces at the end of February, 1871. But then the city rose up, partly inspired by Communists, in defiance of this and other decisions. The revolt was subsequently put down with great bloodshed, forcing many people to flee the country for political reasons, and these events were closely followed in the colonial press.

25 Orestes, son of Agamemnon, slays his mother to revenge the death of his father, and consequently is pursued unrelentingly by the Furies, grim winged ministers of the vengeance of the gods.

26 What he suffers is the mark and fate of Cain, who murdered his brother Abel (Genesis, iv, 1–15), and which symbolise those actions by which humankind confirms its fallen state.

27 *ouvrier en couleurs*, worker in colours. The following French expressions merit explanation or translation: "exposed", a play on words from the verb *exposer* to exhibit; *collier de Vénus*, necklace of Venus; *une tête d'expression*, expressive face; *point de l'inconnu*, the unknown nuance or place, referring both to her hidden charms and their imminent unveiling; "*Monplaisir*", (my pleasure)—signalling clearly what motivates the French aristocrat.

28 Hester Prynne, the heroine of Nathaniel Hawthorne's tale, *The Scarlet Letter*, is condemned to alienation and to wear the letter 'A' for adulteress because of a clandestine liaison. She

bears a child but refuses to name its father, who is a local Puritan minister. She is a victim of male hypocrisy and a focal point for age-old fears of woman as other and uncontrollable.

29 In Vincenzo Bellini's opera *La Sonnambula (The Sleepwalker)* Amina sleepwalks into another man's room and, on being found there, is falsely accused of infidelity. Later, however, she is vindicated, whereupon she sings the famous aria beginning "*Ah! non giunge* . . .", or "Ah! human thought does not reach to the happiness of which I am full".